ANARCHO-SF
SCIENCE FICTION AND THE STATELESS SOCIETY

Edited by Rich Dana

With recent work by
Mick Farren, Nicholas P. Oakley, klipschutz, Ursula Pflug,
Chris Bird, Ben Beck, Davi Barker, F.J. Bergmann, Alou Randon,
Ric Driver and Ricardo Feral

Classic stories by
Philip K. Dick and E.M. Forster

Illustrations by
Tobey A. Anderson, Chris Bird and Blair Gauntt

AnarchoSF V.1:
Science Fiction and The Stateless Society
© 2014 Obsolete Press
obsolete-press.com

ISBN-13:978-1495356025
ISBN-10:1495356027

Cover design and page layouts by Blair Gauntt

For more information about how you can submit work to future volumes
of AnarchoSF, or to purchase, distribute and support future Obsolete!
publications, please write to: anarchosf@riseup.net

CONTENTS

INTRODUCTION
by Rich Dana

Since the earliest days of western literature (and even in the folk tales that preceded it) political commentary has been a part of our storytelling tradition. Popular stories have often reflected the power structure of the times, sometimes criticizing leaders and governments in a way that would never be allowed in journalism or scholarly essays.

Centuries separate the Mother Goose nursery rhymes (which criticized the royalty of Tudor England) and the anarchist visions of science fiction authors like Philip K. Dick and Ursula Le Guin, but in many ways the core motivations remain the same. They are commentaries on "the State." Le Guin herself said "science fiction is not predictive; it is descriptive," rejecting the notion that SF is "about the future". Although some SF readers may be satisfied with the escapism of "space operas," many fans of the genre hold strong political opinions and seek out authors whose work reflects that view.

With roots going back to the early 19th century, science fiction took shape as a 20th century literary movement. At the turn of the century, inexpensive printing technology brought about the rise of popular literature. Western, detective and romance stories all boomed, but SF reflected the times like no other genre. SF developed in the wake of the industrial revolution, rapid mechanization of warfare, and the rise of corporations and statism. Science fiction writers both glorified and criticized all of these aspects of modern society, and fans became vocal participants in the debate.

Much like Futurism and Surrealism, its visual arts counterparts in the early 20th century, science fiction, its writers and fans fell somewhere toward the ends of the spectrum between fascist and marxist camps. Much of the "space opera" fiction of the 1920s onward featured militaristic themes, while much of the utopian work was penned by self-described Trotskyists. Well into the "Golden Age" of science fiction in the 30s and 40s, the debate raged between these opposing camps and their visions of ideal government, although almost no one seemed to be writing about the third way; no government at all.

1

There are some notable exceptions in the early part of the 20th century, primarily works in the dystopian vein that respond to the rapid growth of mega-totalitarian states and the real-world anarchist battle against the onslaught of mechanized corporate-sponsored fascism of the Spanish revolution. Yevgeny Zamyatin's *We* (1920), Aldous Huxley's *Brave New World* (1932) and of course George Orwell's *1984* (1949) all addressed the plight of the individual under the boot heel of the state.

Ayn Rand's *Anthem* (1938) is among the most powerful of the anti-totalitarian SF works of the era, although clearly derivative of Zamyatin. Rand herself dismissed anarchism and she only wrote two novels that could be considered science fiction, her work is a perennial favorite among budding libertarians and anarcho-capitalists. Much misunderstood by leftist detractors and rightist fans alike, Rand's work will continue to draw a bright line between anarcho-capitalists and anarcho-syndicalists for the foreseeable future.

Robert A. Heinlein is another controversial character of the mid twentieth century SF scene. His classic *The Moon is a Harsh Mistress* (1966) is an undeniable high point in Anarcho SF, describing the struggles of a self-described "Rational Anarchist" in a fledgeling lunar society of so-called "loonies." In fact, much of Heinlein's work glorifies the individual in opposition to the state, although some of his themes are highly questionable and have garnered harsh criticisms of racism and sexism. An in-depth look at the high and low points of Heinlein's work is beyond the scope of this article, but a simple analogy might be to compare Heinlein to Ron Paul. Both men came of age in an era and culture in which certain ideas were acceptable that are now considered reprehensible, and in some cases their ideas reflect that. Still, both rose to be outspoken representatives of many of the ideas about which most anarchists agree. Wether to accept or reject their body of work is solely up to the individual reader.

With the late 60s came the rise of what UK radical SF writer Mick Farren described as "the Psychedelic Left," and with that movement came a tsunami of Anarcho SF addressing issues of freedom surrounding everything from race to sexuality, personal drug use to economics. Samuel Delaney, Philip K. Dick and others blazed onto the science fiction scene with a furor of anti-establishmentari-anism. In England, the "New Wave" of SF included Michael Moor-cock and the sublime J.G. Ballard, whose novels like *The Drought* (1964) and *The Atrocity Exhibition* (1969) provided a haunting, in-trospective alternative to the mainstream media vision of society. Ursula K. Le Guin's *The Dispossessed*, published in 1974, uses the SF genre to speculate on how two societies–one based on capitalism and on based on socialism– develop on twin planets.

One of the pillars of the anarcho-libertarian movement of the late 20th century was Robert Anton Wilson, who co-authored the seminal *Illuminatus! Trilogy*. Wilson wrote a handful of novels that fall within a loose definition of SF, along with a plethora of non-fiction work in which he introduced many readers to the ideas of Lysander Spooner, Benjamin Tucker and other important anarcho-libertarians. He introduced the idea of "Guerrilla Ontology"–using his writing to break down limited world views and encouraged pranksterism as a form of direct action.

In the later part of the 20th century, a less experimental, more specifically libertarian theme became popular in SF circles. The Libertarian Futurist Society was formed in the early 1980s, and be-gan presenting the Prometheus Award in 1982. Winners have in-cluded greats like F. Paul Wilson, Larry Niven and Poul Anderson. Alongside this more mainstream libertarian movement came Cyber-punk, the edgy, dystopian vision of Darwinian technology. William Gibson, Bruce Sterling and Rudy Rucker rose from the cyberpunk pack. The 80's also brought about a new wave of what might be loosely described as "anarcha-feminist" novels. Margaret Atwood's *A Handmaid's Tale* and the works of Octavia Butler explore the struggle of women against the oppression of religious and patriar-chal societies.

A wonderful book from 1989 is perhaps the quintessential An-archo-SF anthology. *Semiotext(e)SF* was edited by anarchist writer Peter Lamborn Wilson (Hakim Bey), Rudy Rucker and Robert An-ton Wilson and features a who's who of late-century counterculture science fiction writers including Gibson, Sterling and Ballard, along with Paul DiFillipo, Philip Jose Farmer, Colin Wilson and many more.

Most recently, Kim Stanley Robinson, Neal Stephenson, Cory Doctorow and others have covered the spectrum of anarchist visions from dystopian to utopian. Doctorow's young adult novels like *Little Brother* (2008), Pirate Cinema (2012) and *Homeland* (2013) are particularly important for introducing the ideas of personal freedom and opposition to state control to younger readers.

Any discussion of science fiction and it's place in western culture would be incomplete without mentioning the role of "Fandom" and "Con Culture". The time and place of the first "Con" (convention) of SF fans is the subject of some debate, but organized groups of science fiction readers were most certainly meeting as early as 1935. From those early meetings up to the present, Cons are almost a textbook definition of what Peter Lamborn Wilson described as a TAZ (Temporary Autonomous Zone). In most cases with minimal hierarchical government and minimal rules, SF fans converge and openly share work, conduct commerce and interact around common interests and common goals. Unlike any other genre of literature, a completely unregulated system is in place by which fans are often allowed–and in some cases encouraged–to write "in the universe" of other professional writers, creating their own stories utilizing established characters and settings. In many cases, SF writers come from the ranks of fandom, being promoted in a merit-based system rather than through an academic or corporate structure like other forms of literature. In many ways, SF "Fandom" can be seen as a precursor to "Open Source" culture, and because there are so many SF fans among the ranks of "nerds" and "computer geeks," it would not be a hard case to prove.

In 2009, the self professed marxist SF writer China Mieville came out with an anthology of Marxist influence science fiction entitled *Red Planets*. It's an excellent book, but it represents a look backward, an examination of noble ideas of a flawed, 20th century philosophy. SF readers and writers have always represented the cutting edge of cultural thought, and it is time to focus on the work of those that celebrate the inevitable step forward into a culture beyond the violent confines of "the state" toward peaceful self-government.

This first volume of *AnarchoSF* features stories that address anarchy, anarchism and the stateless society. It includes recent work by young writers as well as veterans, along with classic anarchist-inspired work in the SF genre.

A note about future volumes: Obsolete Press is accepting submissions for future volumes of the *AnarchoSF* anthology series as of April, 2014.

As you might have noticed on the cover, we are using a five pointed star of black, white, green, red, yellow, purple and pink to represent the major contemporary schools of anarchist thought. White for anarcho-pacifism, green for anarcho-environmentalism, red for anarcho-syndicalism, yellow for anarcho-capitalism, purple for anarcha-feminism and pink for Queer anarchism. Black stands for the common goals of all anarchists. I have devised this symbol to represent what I like to call "The New Futurians" –SF and speculative fiction writers who are actively criticism statism though their writing and exploring the outcomes of statism, or presenting alternatives to it.

Our goal is to present future volumes that feature stories that focus on the themes of white, red, yellow, purple, pink and green anarchism. Each will feature recent work from emerging authors and artists as well as classic stories.

For more information about deadlines, how you can submit work or purchase, distribute and support future issues, please write to:

anarchosf@riseup.net

Obsolete Press
POB 72
Victor, IA
52347

BLAIR GAUNTT

DEDICATION:
MICK FARREN, 1943-2013

On the night of July 23rd, 2013, Mick Farren took the stage at a London club with his longtime bandmates, The Deviants. He was not feeling well, and sat on a stool to perform the first few songs. Then, with the rock and roll ringing in his ears, he collapsed and died. Just short of his 70th birthday, the science fiction novelist, gonzo journalist, proto-punk anarchist prankster and sometimes rock and roll vocalist died with his boots on. It shocked everyone, but nobody was surprised. Most agreed that he had lived a charmed life, and that his epic penchant for cigarettes and booze could have killed five younger men.

I met Mick in 1986. I had recently moved to New York from New Orleans, via Berlin. I was working at Forbidden Planet, the science fiction and comics shop on Broadway in the Village. I was already familiar with Mick's writing, having read his "Phaid the Gambler" and "DNA Cowboys" books, so when my roommate, Vicky Rose, told me she was playing bass in Mick's new band, Tijuana Bible, I was impressed. I tagged along to gigs, acting as an ad hoc roadie and sponging free beers.

Mick was great on stage–a ranting rockabilly street-preacher with the eloquence of an Oxford lecturer. Off stage he could be surly, with a cutting dry wit, but he was also a charming and generous guy on many occasions. During my first snowy, dead-broke winter in NYC, I would eat rice and beans in a cuban diner on 2nd Ave in the East Village, then cross the street to nurse a cheap beer and play video games with my buddy Don Rock at the Mars Bar. On numerous occasions, the side door would open, snow blowing in like a scene from a movie, and Mick would enter, wrapped in his long black duster. He would join us at the bar, buy a couple of rounds of Rolling Rocks and talk radical politics, rock and roll, cult movies, whatever.

I lost contact with Mick, but never stopped following his work. Twenty years passed before I started OBSOLETE! Magazine, but I knew I wanted Mick in the first issue. I sheepishly contacted him

7

through his blog, Doc40, and asked him if I could reprint one of his older stories. He wrote back and said that I was welcome to, but he would much prefer to write a new piece for me. I was thrilled! Mick had been the editor of *The International Times*, one of the world's premiere underground newspapers. Mick had been arrested for obscenity over publishing underground comics, represented himself against the white-wigged barristers of the Old Bailey–AND WON. Mick had been at the Battle for Grovesnor Square in 1968 and organized the legendary Phun City Festival. He was the real deal, and he wanted to write for my fucked up little anarchist art and lit paper.

He was featured several times in OBSOLETE!, and had written the first of what was to be a series of regular stream of consciousness rants. We were communicating regularly, and working on the idea for this book. The last email I received from him was as follows:

> *"Your email makes me very happy. I have been playing with this style (I feel like it's inventing literary bebop) but all the time there's the nagging doubt that I may actually be crazy. Please, go ahead and run it. I've come far enough with this stuff that there would be no problem sustaining it as a series. This book of yours sounds extremely interesting. I think when some strange force drags a book off course you have to go with it and see what happens. It won't get you in good with Random House, but it may it may be the conception of something really interesting. Which is what it's really all about. (Unless you want a Ferrari.) My partner Annmarie got the (OBSOLETE!) baseball shirt. She likes it, despite the (bile yellow) color...*
>
> *In other news, I have another novel in the oven. It's a short novel, maybe 45,000 words, to keep costs down. The title is "Atlas Turned Off The TV" and spans a spectrum of characters from John Galt's grandson to The Creature From The Black Lagoon. I figure in maybe a month I'll have enough to show you.*
>
> *I must now watch the TV news...*
>   *All the best,*
>   *Mick---"*

I did not hear from Mick again.

That last piece, *What is your Problem, Agent X9?,* appeared in OBSOLETE! #8 and is reprinted in this book. Unfortunately, there will be no more in the series. I still hope to read the manuscript for *Atlas Turned Off The TV* one day.

This first volume of *AnarchoSF* is dedicated to Mick Farren. It could not be dedicated to anyone else.

WHAT IS YOUR PROBLEM, AGENT X9?

by Mick Farren

"The very planet proves to be alive. And very pissed off."

The report on you is filed, my friend. You, Agent X9, above all others, should realize that the data cannot be reversed. The algorithms of the Corporate Hegemony are inflexible. The images are graven. They rule with cool and absolute binary authority. The database may only be amended and items only added to the labyrinths of detail and the profiles that stretch to the edge of entropy. The report has been filed Agent X9. It has joined the endless and ultimately personal catalogues of caprices and conceits. A major responsibility of the Intelligence Committee of the Corporate Hegemony is to preserve the minutiae of peccadillo and purchase, intimacies and indiscretions and store them on the mainframes in those mines measureless to man. It is a vital foundation of the Sociopath Agenda. You were once one of our most respected Continental Operatives. As such you should be aware that absolutely nothing is reversible. All structures are indistinguishable one for another in infinite reflection, standardized by electric dissection and quantified by template. You are Damned Agent X9. That's how they would have expressed it in the ancient days. What's that? You want a cigarette? The general regulations specify this as a non-smoking facility but here in the white room we might make an exception. Will someone fetch Agent X9 a cigarette and the means with which to light it?

The report is filed, Agent X9. Smoke your cigarette and reflect how the requirement is helplessness. The requirement has always been helplessness. Not only from the victim but from the victor. Our drones release death from the above. They fall free from a clear blue sky. They do not consider the merits of the mission or contemplate its morality. They are merely machines. The same could be said of the machines air-conditioned operators deep in their protected bunkers. They perform their assigned tasks. They calibrate for assigned targets. They are compliant. They obey. They do not question. In fact they strive for excellence in what they do. They believe the infallibility of their instructions. Remember the good Colonel Benton? "I feel no emotional attachment to the enemy. I have a duty, and I execute the duty." You also believed Agent X9. When you were sent against the Hello Kitty subversion, the Deathless Men, The Horst Wessel Brigade or the Ancients of Lhasa you also complied with discussion or argument. What happened, Agent X9? When did you develop this philosophical schizophrenia? In former times, when you stood in hall of mirrors and the Lady from Shanghai opened fire, you ducked the shining shards and carried out your mission. What changed, Agent X9?

Before the battle of Passchendaele a British general issued an order, "Maps must conform to plans and not plans to maps. Facts that interfered with plans were impertinencies." The Intelligence Committee may not totally agree with this concept, but it certainly has its historical merits in that it is plainly a forerunner of modern thinking by the Corporate Hegemony what would ultimately find form in the Sociopath Agenda. The mass must move as one with a driven uniformity. For each to plot an individual course would create the abject chaos of uncharted anarchy. Law enforcement fills the prisons. It is their vocation. They are not required to reason why, just fill their quota. The sick die. The poor starve. The churches preach insanity. The advertising industry creates impossible desires and implausible expectations. Tolerance is eliminated and fear is substituted. The pliable iron is set in the soul of men. You have done your part in establishing that program, Agent X9. Ignorance has been nurtured and nourished. Pornography is encouraged. Paranoia is cultivated. The underclass is publicized as the ever-lurking threat. There but for the grace of consumption go you and go I. Their internecine criminality and territorial gang violence is tacitly fostered as a means of intimidation. Their drug traffic is clandestinely regulated and monitored to keep them within the designated boundaries by psycho-chemical manipulation. Education has now fully collapsed on itself and the children remain feral, but eruptions are managed and the destruction is confined to their own habitats. They burn their own turf. The body count is media fodder. The sub-culture is exploitable. Function is inflexible. Function is always inflexible.

Did you forget that Agent X9 when you flaunted your new found individualism? Individuality can only be the prerogative of a tiny and elevated elite and, even then, it must be subject to multiple and geometric restrictions. Public postures of leadership and pri-

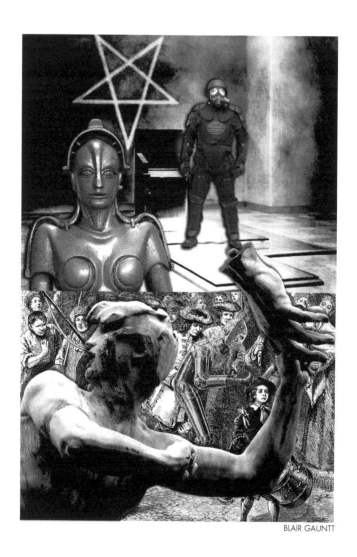

BLAIR GAUNTT

vate poses of decadence among this quasi-elite are as narrowly proscribed as the tailored delusions of the masses. They are permitted their gaudy party favors, their garish notoriety, and extravagant illusions of superiority, their deviant sex and their own costly and rarified varieties of recreation drugs. They are dazzled by their own glitter, their metallic eyelashes, and the contents of their gift bags. They are encouraged to amass their toys, their mansions, their yachts and their jets, to consume beyond reason, and leave their vast carbon tire tracks. They are conditioned to strive for fortunes so inflated they are abstractions. They are taught a magical arithmetic and a numerical concept of the elemental self-esteem. They are reminded how they are bright candles but the wind is always waiting.

Even we on the Intelligence Committee do not attempt to think for ourselves. The very fabric of our society dictates that all levels adhere at all times to the essential construction of the Corporate Hegemony and the Sociopath Agenda. But you, Agent X9, have elected to think for yourself. You have embraced a condition is wholly singular, when, at the very least only the binary is recognized and only the totality is accessible or acceptable. You appear to believe you are the recipient of a revelation. You imagine you have seen the error of our ways. You have attempted to apply logic where logic is inapplicable. You make the essential mistake of believing that humanity as a species can be saved. As long ago as 1949, the great Harry Lime notably remarked, "Nobody thinks in terms of human beings. Would you really feel any pity if one of those dots stopped moving forever?" You ignore the crucial tipping point after which humanity became fully viral and its general survival became unworthy of consideration except in small and carefully selected superior enclaves. As for the rest, it is unfortunate. As a virus they are a destructive infection of the overall biosphere and only worthy of elimination. The choice is not easy but it has been made, and that choice is the core of the Sociopath Agenda.

So you see, Agent X9, any misguided attempts you might make to save humanity or civilization as we know it are far too little and their lateness defies contemplation.

Your sorry attempt to forge a treasonous liaison with the Daughters of Gaia only serves to demonstrate your unqualified misinterpretation of the cybernetic feedback systems operated unconsciously by the biota. You linger in the 20th century. Agent X9. Once upon a time, the Corporate Hegemony assumed itself a total odds with the Lovelock proposal. They too saw no alternative to preserving humanity if only as producer/consumers. It was only when the emergent Intelligence Committee presented evidence of how human beings in their current numbers were inimical to the broad stabilization of the conditions of habitability in a full homeostasis that the higher thinking began to change. Our masters accepted that this world of humans is dying, Agent X9. They accepted it very easily. Parts of it are already dead. They cannot be resuscitated. Our only option was to maintain a semblance of order as the systems fail. It was the only alternative with which to retain power. The Corporate Hegemony was well aware they were the descendants of all feudal lords, warrior chieftains, violent dictators, and totalitarian butchers of old. In their form at the time of the tipping point they were opportunists motivated by self-interest and greed, and inclined to dominate or subjugate those around them through manipulative means. A new order needed to evolve from the previous policies of destructive self-interest.

We have no Cossacks, no pogroms, no purges, and no final solution. The secret police operate primarily for their own amusement. Humanity will be largely destroyed but we are not the destroyers per se. Lovelock himself made it clear. "The Earth System behaves as a single, self-regulating procedure with physical, chemical, biological, and human components". The Earth's survival depends on the interaction of living forms with inorganic elements and one of those living forms is now too degraded to be part of the interaction. The human component has grievously malfunctioned and Earth will eliminate it. The Earth itself will destroy humanity. That makes your failed alliance with the Daughters of Gaia all the more ironic. The very planet proves to be alive. And very pissed off. It will push man to extinction. The Corporate Hegemony may help speed the process in some small ways. An epidemic here. A famine there. A withdrawal of aid. A nuclear accident or a toxic cloud. The Earth will do the rest. It will throw off viral humanity. It will cure itself with earthquakes and volcanoes, fire and flood, climate shift, and things at which we can only guess. Our own minor efforts are what might be called transactional. We sacrifice our own kind in return for exceedingly limited numbers of us being allowed to continue as what might call living fossils. A tiny percentage of the former species world given sanctuary in protected enclaves from which we guarantee we will not spread and cause no more harm to planet. In this we embrace the largest possible picture. The Sociopath Agenda is, at root, an acceptance that humanity has outgrows any possible usefulness, and we are making what we can from its demise. Didn't I make clear that the Corporate Hegemony was a coterie of advanced whores and evolved opportunists?

But what of you Agent X9. We on the Intelligence Committee are not the frivolous or gratuitous torturers of old. Pain is not our entertainment or distraction. Your life will merely be concluded as painlessly as possible because, knowing all that you know you cannot be allowed to persist, world at an end. Would care for another cigarette, Agent X9? And perhaps a blindfold?

Nicholas P. Oakley *is a speculative fiction author from Inverness, Scotland. His short stories have been published in Interstellar Fiction, Wily Writers, Mad Scientist Journal, and Andromeda Spaceways. His first SF novel, The Watcher, is available from the anarchist See Sharp Press. He blogs at http://quercusrubra.co.uk.*

RAG AND BONE

by Nicholas P. Oakley

"No need for that," Felix said across the open channel. "You had plenty of warning." The hull beeped its displeasure at him again, the laser fire dancing across the thick, scarred armour plating. "Look, cut it out. Figure you in enough trouble as it is."

The answer was about the usual. Felix allowed himself a tired smile, zoning out the rant with a gesture. He didn't really blame them. If he were in their position, he'd be just as pissed.

As the man raved on, Felix brought up the itinerary. He wasn't concerned by the weapons fire. The laser was nothing more than a pea shooter for taking out small meteoroids, and certainly no threat to him. Felix looked at the list of jobs. Four more places to clear today. The schedule was getting tougher. There used to be a time when he'd do one of these a week, but things had changed. His employer's patience had worn thin. They were tired of the endless appeals, the protests. It was getting violent, too. Felix's junker was one of the most heavily armoured ships in the inner system. These days it had to be.

Felix unmuted the link, the man's expletive-ridden diatribe filling the cockpit once more. Felix glanced at the clock. Still five minutes until the deadline. Even with so many jobs on – he'd already done three this shift – he still liked to get to the jobs early. Seemed fairer, somehow. He knew guys in the business who'd just pull up and do the job without even a warning, then blast off to the next one. Felix didn't like to do things that way. It didn't seem professional. Or courteous.

The man on the other end of the link seemed to be running out of imaginative things to say about Felix's late mother. Felix knew that the countdown broadcast his ship's AI had been sending out since he'd arrived would be a distraction. Even the most defiant of them struggled to be imaginative when their computer systems were going haywire with false reports of life support systems failing and airlocks malfunctioning.

Still, the majority of them waited until the absolute last moment, as if not quite believing that their homes, their entire existence, was about to get snuffed out. That all those unpaid bills, court warnings, and threats were finally becoming a reality. That they really did have to get the hell out or get junked along with their habitats.

The countdown was nearly over. Felix never kept the line open for the last hundred seconds. Too many noises there that could keep a man from sleeping.

His thumb hovered over the terminate button, but, just as he was about to push it and cut the line, a horrible noise stopped him. A young girl, crying.

His thumb hesitated, betraying him despite his best instincts. The crying stopped, and Felix could hear a low murmuring. Then she started to speak.

"My dad says he- we can't afford to pay you but that he's really sorry. I know he is, he's been really sad since he lost his job..." Her voice trailed off, and Felix could hear the man whispering something. "He says to tell you that we're not going to leave and- and we don't have anywhere to go so you go right ahead and do what you have to do but we'll be staying- But please, if you could just give us a few more..."

Felix finally regained control of his morbidly curious thumb and cut the transmission. Damn, he thought. She can't have been more than eight or nine. He hated the man for putting her up to it, but he knew he should have cut the line straight away. It was his own fault. Why the hell didn't they just leave, why did they always stick around hoping for the best? They all knew what happened out here when you couldn't pay the rent. Space was expensive, and these habitat modules costs a fortune, worth a lot to people like his employer.

But would you leave? a voice in his head said, perhaps the same one that had control of his thumb a moment before.

Space was expensive, but it was safe. Clean. If you could afford the rent, you could live without fear here, without worrying what germs people were breathing on you on the metro, without worrying about your kids getting stolen out of school in broad daylight, worrying about the gangs or the drugs or the violence or the water. Given a choice between there and here, well, Felix could see that there wasn't any choice about it at all.

The countdown had expired whilst Felix had been having that familiar, uncomfortable discussion with himself. That made him feel sick. He hoped the family in the habitat he was about to impound hadn't noticed. What could be worse than the last-minute reprieve snatched away?

Felix's fingers were a sudden flurry of motion as he tapped and gestured to begin the capture procedure. He felt the shudder through his chair as the cargo hold door began its wide yawn below him. The computer replaced its warning broadcast that had been scrambling the habitats systems with the real thing. The life support systems really did tick off this time, the airlock seals disengaged, and the lifepods jettisoned.

Felix manually guided the junker closer to the habitat module. It was smaller than most, a simple four-pod one-family setup, and from the looks of it, expensive to run. Too small to produce much of its own food or water, and not much in the way of solar capture either. Felix gestured and the docking clamps stretched out, grappling the habitat and reeling it in. When it was safely nestled inside the cargohold, the dismantling bots began their work, yellow and green flashes on Felix's HUD indicating their progress.

The job almost complete, Felix flipped a switch and starting prepping the ship's massive fusion engines. From the corner of his eye he saw the blinking icon representing one of the jettisoned lifepods on the interface in front of him, a small SOS beacon transmitting in weak bursts. He doubted they had any rescue insurance, but that wasn't his employer's concern, so it wasn't his, either. Few of them bothered with the lifepods, preferring to die in their homes at the junker's hands over the slow asphyxiation in those cramped little pods. Felix didn't blame them.

Just as the engines began their final ignition sequence, Felix rotated his palm over one of the lifepods where it appeared on the HUD, scanning it more closely, checking for thermal signatures.

There were none.

Felix gunned the engines, roaring away from the scene like a hit and run driver, palms sweaty and mouth dry.

#

He hadn't always done this. No, back in the early days, he'd actually enjoyed his job. It was one he felt comfortable talking about in public, one that didn't provoke wary looks, didn't induce guilt-ridden dreams. No, before, people used to like him, even appreciate what he did for a living.

Deep-space colonization was a disaster. The distances were just too great. The human psyche was simply unable to cope, and, at the time, the engineering proficiency required to make it more tolerable was far beyond humanity. This was back before space hangars or cryo, where the only spaceships were cramped little compartments bolted together, where prospective adventurers slept toe-to-toe, hurtling toward the darkness in tin cans at a rate slower even than Felix's two-hundred-year-old behemoth of a junker.

It wasn't just the psychological problems those first explorers and colonists encountered, the catastrophic bouts of psychosis, of suicidal melancholy, of existential despair, and murderous rage that ended so many of the deep-space missions. It seemed that if something could go wrong, something could break or melt or combust, it invariably would. Radiation leaks, faulty equipment, haywire AI, explosive oxygen recyclers. All these and more filled the papers and feeds on Earth with alarming, and discouraging, frequency.

And there was something quite terrifying about space that anyone that had been past, say, Mars, could tell you about in vivid detail. Getting and staying away from the space around Earth was far easier said than done.

So when the Earth became increasingly inhospitable, and when the tech for space colonization – the self-contained habitat modules in particular – became industrialized and within reach of more and more citizens of Earth, those looking for a new life didn't stray far. They were quite content to live in the space around Earth itself, the perils of deep space colonization too great a hurdle for the majority.

That's where Felix came in. It was was all very well for these newly-enfranchised settlers planning to start afresh around Earth, but that space was already occupied, of sorts. Occupied by debris. Trillions and trillions of pieces of space junk.

Felix was a binman in space, a trawlerman whose catch was the centuries of crap human civilization had seen fit to dump on its ill-fated trips to the stars. Satellites, abandoned space stations, telescopes, even radioactive waste and caskets of human remains. Whatever their origin, whatever their former purpose or composition, they had to make way, and, with Felix's help, they did. Felix and his kind opened up the way for these new colonists, opened the path to a new life in space, allowed them their dreams.

And now he quite literally crushed them.

#

Felix guided the junker into the cavernous station owned by CPB, the collection agency he worked for. They were by far the biggest agency working space repossession, and owned four of these stations, all equally vast and in space usually reserved for the very richest. Debt collection was a lucrative business.

Felix didn't hang around for long. Most of the station was an unwelcoming place, full of labyrinthine corridors leading to vast hangars and disassembly lines, all Spartan functionality and exposed industry. It was like being in a giant factory, and Felix never felt entirely at ease on these decks.

Jaime was already in the bar, sitting at a table, his only company a half-empty bottle of whisky. Felix and he lived together, but only had a single needlecraft for commuting, and, as booze was cheaper than taxis, Jaime often waited for Felix's shift to end before riding home together.

"Hey brother. Drink before we head off?"

"Sure, why not," said Felix, sitting down. The bar was big, and few of the tables were occupied, so they were able to talk without being overheard.

"One of them days?" Jaime asked as he poured Felix a drink.

"Aye, one of them. You?"

"Same. Park was here earlier. Had quite a day herself."

"Oh?"

"Yeah. One of those immolation jobs everyone's been talking about. Three families, about a minute before their time was up."

"Not good."

"Nope. Napalm, then a timed explosion. Only, they filmed it."

"They what?"

"Filmed themselves doing it. Park showed it to me. They

broadcast it to her. You see this feller lighting up his whole family, kids screaming and begging as their skin crisps over. It's disgusting. I almost puked to watch it. The guy, the dad I guess, he was looking at the person holding the camera the whole time. Man, Felix, he wasn't saying shit. Just staring as he did it. Then he starts covering himself with the jelly, then whoosh. Lights it up himself. Really creepy."

"How's Park?"

"Shook up. She didn't really have much time to think about it, 'cause of the explosives. She had to get it in the hold and neutralized pronto. But she... CPB gave her a week's bonus and a couple of shifts off. She came by to buy everyone drinks." Jaime picked up the bottle of whisky, sloshing the brown contents around inside. "Courtesy of her."

They had a couple of shots in silence. Felix smoked his pipe whilst Jaime re-read the bottle's label.

"What we gonna do?" Jaime asked, suddenly.

"Do?"

"Yeah. You know. These immolation things."

"Guess it's just part of the job now."

"I'm not sure I- I still haven't been sleeping Fe. The dreams-"

"You try that stuff I got ya?"

"Yeah, it didn't help none. No better than this," Jaime said, draining his shot glass.

"You could try what the others do. You know, just turn up on the dot, play the recording, then do the job."

"I been doing that for weeks. And I stopped checking the life-pods well before that. I still know, you know? I can't pretend any more." His voice was quiet, almost a whisper. "It ain't right bro. We gotta get out of this. Find something else."

"Like what?"

"Anything. Haulage. Freighters or something. Anything. Where we don't got to-"

Felix interrupted him. "Someone else would take our place if we did. There's plenty who'd kill for our jobs, all the benefits."

"Fuck the benefits," Jaime said, too loudly. A few heads turned, so he went on in a quieter voice. "Fuck the benefits, Fe. We is murdering them. You and me both know it ain't right. We killing our own. People like you and me. That could be us out there if one of us got sick or something."

Felix took a long sip of his pipe. It was true. The tiny habitat they shared took nearly all their combined wage packets in rent, even though Earth was just a small marble in the distance and there was barely enough space to stand up in the whole place.

"I'm not sure I can be part of it no more," Jaime said.

Felix said nothing for a while, thinking. "Quitting ain't the answer," he said, finally.

"What you mean?"

"I mean, if we want to stop this, change things, make it right so that dads aren't torching their kids because they lost their jobs, then quitting is the last thing we should be doing."

"What then?"

Felix poured himself another shot, then downed it in one, savouring the burning sensation in his chest. "We gotta fight."

#

Park shared a habitat with her extended family. Mom and dad, four brothers and their families. Plenty of kids. Their habitat was nice. Felix had heard that one of her brothers did something vaguely managerial. They were all out now though, all except Park and the kids. Even her elderly parents still worked.

Felix and Jaime were sat across from Park in the central module. The kids played noisily around them, enjoying the novelty of having her home and the strange smells of tobacco, alcohol, and sweat that surrounded her guests.

"Hear you had quite a day today," Felix said.

"You could say that. That why you're here?"

"Yeah. Sorry to call unannounced like that."

"No problem. Can I get you fellers a drink?"

Felix shook his head. "We've come to talk to you about the immolation job. About the transmission, the video, they sent. You still have it?"

"Why?"

Jaime fidgeted in his seat. "We want to use it," he said.

Park frowned. "Use it for what?" she said, warily.

"No, nothing like that," said Felix. "We ain't sadists. But we're thinking it might be useful if a few more people got to see that video."

"People like who?"

"Well it doesn't really matter who. Just people. Figure if enough people see that then we-"

"What? That it'll change their minds about all this?" She laughed unpleasantly. "You two are so naïve. Everyone already knows this kinda shit goes on. They hate the agency more than anything already."

"Yes, but if we-" said Jaime.

Park carried on, ignoring him. "But the agency are clever. People hate them, us, but everyone knows that it's gotta be done. Just like war or taxes. It's inevitable. Earth is bursting at the seams, space is packed, and there ain't all that much of it. At least much of it that people want to live in. Those that can't pay for the privilege any longer have to make room for those than can."

"You believe that?" asked Felix.

"Yes. No. Oh, I don't know." She slumped back into her chair.

"Don't know about you, Park, but we've had enough. Reckon there had to be another way of doing things. One that doesn't involving roasted children. We've been talking, and-"

"What can you two possibly do?"

"Well, for one, we can release that recording. Let everyone see for themselves the price they pay, how desperate these people are."

"What then? Billions of people live out here, and there must be a couple of thousand corps who own the space out here. Even if you convince a few junkers at CPB to throw it in, they'll just replace you, or hire someone else to do the job."

Felix shook his head. "Way it looks to me, someone scrapes up the cash to get out here and get themselves a hab, then no-one got the right to charge or kick them out for the privilege of being there. No-one can own space, at least in my book."

Park took a sip of coffee, looking between the two men seated opposite her. "No. Think about it. It'd just be anarchy. Everyone on Earth would just rush right out here if you abolish the space rights, get rid of the rental agreements. We'd be overrun out here."

Felix cocked his head. One of the children was weaving in and out between the chairs they were sitting on, squealing with delight at being chased by some unseen pursuer. "I reckon we let other people figure out what happens after, how we organize things. Maybe we go a bit deeper into space, maybe be build bigger habs, as big as the agency's hangar. Don't see why not. But I don't really care about that right now. All I care about is stopping people frying their whole families and sabotaging their homes 'cause they can't pay the rent to some corp who says they got some piece of paper saying they already own the space. That ain't right."

Felix paused, and looked pointedly at the kid, who was trying to hide between his legs. Felix stuck a thumb towards the boy. "Do I really need to say more?"

Park sat for a long time in silence. Felix held her stare. Then, finally, she nodded and took out a small pocket video player. She tossed it across the room to him.

"Thanks," he said as he caught it.

"You're doing the right thing Park," said Jaime.

"What you going to do afterwards, after you broadcast it?" she said.

Felix rose, beckoning to Jaime that they were leaving.

"We'll figure something out."

#

The junkers moved with surprising alacrity as the hostile ship burned towards the habitat. A torpedo left the frigate almost the moment it was in range, but the junkers' defenses were quicker, and they rapidly deployed counter-measures along the torpedoes path and moved to intercept the oncoming hostile ship.

Felix released the grappler. The AI had calculated the shot perfectly, and the sharp hooks plunged into the frigate's side. As Felix began reeling it in, the smaller ship let off everything it had at him. Uranium-capped torpedoes and laser arrays pummeled the junker's hulking mass in an enormous barrage. But his junker could take it, had taken much more than this. Soon the junker's gaping maw swallowed up the wasp-like frigate, digesting its vicious meal and silencing her weapons for good.

Felix's interface lit up with a call. Another plea for help.

Bringing up the strategic overlay, he co-ordinated with the war council and, after a brief discussion, assigned two nearby junkers to intercept. They should make it in time, if the intel on the merc frigates was correct. They were just a couple of the thousands of ships posted around Earth, ready to intervene at a moment's notice.

The transmission had only been the start. Felix had waited two weeks after he left Park's hab with the recording. Two hectic weeks to prepare for its release, to organist, to work out who would follow them, and who wouldn't. Jaime had helped, as had Park, who became an effective, persuasive voice for their cause.

It was surprisingly easy. Even those that Felix had always distrusted, the professionals who didn't seem to give a thought past their paycheck, once Park had bought them a couple of drinks and pushed the right buttons – family, religion, freedom, rewards, whatever it was for them – most of them came over to their side.

In the end their hand was forced. Someone talked. The agency got wind of it. It was hit and miss right up to the last sympathetic junker pilot undocked from the hangars, and even then it looked like it wouldn't be enough. Too many scabs to break the strike.

But they had most of the ships, and what started as a strike soon transformed into something else entirely. The space owners took things into their own hands, hiring mercs to collect the payments the CPB agency and their striking junkers no longer could.

The junkers responded. There was a declaration. The union wouldn't stand by and watch any longer. Anyone who couldn't pay their rent and asked for help would get all the protection the union could provide.

The junker ships didn't have any offensive weapons, but what they lacked in firepower they more than made up in bulk. And, as the strike-turned-resistance grew, more ships came to their side, yearning to throw the yoke of the leeching space-owning corps off their backs. They soon had a fully-fledged navy ready to resist.

That was the catalyst. More and more stopped paying, seeing the impunity the junker navy provided those that no longer could afford or wanted to pay. The owners' early frustration at lost revenue turned to desperation that they had a revolution on their hands. What started as a strike had evolved into an all out war.

Bounties were placed, mercs paid by the number of resisting

habitats they destroyed. This was no longer about rental contracts or late payment. The owners were out to enforce their property rights with all the might money could muster.

Felix's HUD lit up with another call, this time from the habitat he'd just saved from annihilation at the hands of the merc frigate now being dismantled and crushed in his cargo hold. He thumbed accept. A faint smile played on his lips as the torrent of gratitude filled the cockpit. That never got old.

It would be a long struggle, but it would be worth it.

END

klipschutz is the pen name of Kurt Lipschutz of San Francisco, whose most recent collection is This Drawn & Quartered Moon. He has recently completed the genre-bending worlds linger. Poems have appeared in Poetry (of Chicago), Ambit (U.K.) and The Shop (Ireland), and zines (notably Lee Thorn's FUCK!), as well as anthologies, including The Outlaw Bible of American Poetry. His journalism includes a monograph on Bill Knott, and a comprehensive two-part interview with Carl Rakosi. He is the co-writer of Chuck Prophet's critically acclaimed 2012 release Temple Beautiful.

PROTECT THE QUARTERBACK

by klipschutz

2017: Manhattan, a prison
for the beast-marked and forgotten,
real estate, ha!, hundred foot
electric walls. Mayday! Sabotage!
The President's plane is down
inside, his whereabouts unknown. . .
Bonfires revelate upended hulks,
machine age marvels canted
in postures of obeisance
to resurrected unforgiving gods.
Flesheaters rise from manholes,
roam deracinated streets,
ward off the megastench,
rat-men skitter-squealing in the gloom.

An outlaw w/eyepatch, a war hero gone wrong,
is sent in to bring the President out safe.
Equipped with a snake tattoo [black],
one facial expression [sneer], and firepower,
"Snake" proceeds to walk through sheets of flame,
leaving carnage, Truth, and smoking trim behind.
Free World intact, in high disgust
he saunters off, alone.

Boy stuff, to be sure, roadkill
for the this-means-that-inclined.
But drive-in fare, pre-chick flicks,
has morphed to dysto-camp
ankle deep in a new century
where prisons-for-profit
sprout like mandrake root.
In GQ, the pirate look is back,
and snakes laze by the roadside
in the Arizona sun, threatening no one.
The Free World Order rockets on,
the Bridge To Nowhere Tour. . .

Don't look now, Bill Gates is adjusting his patch—
he's going in, to reconfigure your C drive.

Ursula Pflug *is author of the critically acclaimed novels Green Mu-*
sic (Edge/Tesseract) and The Alphabet Stones (Blue Denim), and
the story collections After The Fires (Tightrope) and Harvesting the
Moon (PS). Her stories have been published in Canada, the US and
the UK, in Fantasy, Strange Horizons, PostScripts, Lady Church-
ill's Rosebud Wristlet and many more. Pflug has been shortlisted
or nominated for the Sunburst Award, the Aurora Award, the Push-
cart Prize, the 3 Day Novel Contest, the Descant Novella Award,
the KM Hunter Award and others. Her work has been funded by
The Ontario Arts Council, the Canada Council for the Arts and The
Laidlaw Foundation.

Pflug has published nonfiction in NOW, Mix Magazine, YYZ, The
Peterborough Examiner, The New York Review of Science Fiction,
Strange Horizons and other publications. She has collaborated ex-
tensively on multi-disciplinary projects with dancers, sculptors, the-
atre and installation artists and film-makers. She has served on the
executive of arts boards including SFCanada, and has worked as an
editor for The Peterborough Review, Takeout, The Link and private
clients. Her first edited book, the fundraiser anthology They Have
To Take You In (HBP) is forthcoming in 2014. She teaches creative
writing at Loyalist College. http://ursulapflug.ca

THE WATER MAN

by Ursula Pflug

The water man came today. I waited all morning, and then all afternoon, painting plastic soldiers to pass the time. Red paint too in the sky when he finally showed; I turned the outside lights on for him and held the door while he carried the big bottles in. He set them all in a row just inside the storm door; there wasn't any other place to put them. When he was done he stood catching his breath, stamping his big boots to warm his feet. Melting snow made little muddy lakes on the linoleum. I dug in my jeans for money to tip him with, knowing I wouldn't find any. Finally I just offered him water.

We drank together. It was cool and clean and good, running down our throats in the dimness of the store. It made me feel wide and quiet, and I watched his big eyes poke around Synapses, checking us out, and while they did, mine snuck a peek at him. He was big and round, and all his layers of puffy clothes made him seem rounder still, like a black version of the Michelin man. He unzipped his parka and I could see a name, Gary, stitched in red over the pocket of his blue coverall. I still didn't have a light on; usually I work in the dark, save the light bill for Deb. But I switched it on when he coughed and he smiled at that, like we'd shared a joke. He had a way of not looking right at you or saying much, but somehow you still knew what he was thinking. Like I knew that he liked secrets, and talking without making sounds. It was neat.

Seemed to me it was looking water–a weird thought out of nowhere–unless it came from him. He seemed to generate them; like he could stand in the middle of a room and in everyone's minds, all around him, weird little thoughts would start cropping up–like that one. My tummy sloshing I looked too, and seemed to see through his eyes and not just mine. Through his I wasn't sure how to take it: a big dim room haunted by dinosaurs. All the junk of this century comes to rest at Synapses; it gets piled to the ceilings and covered with dust. If it's lucky it makes a Head; weird Heads are going to be the thing for Carnival this year, just as they were last, and Debbie's are the best. Her finished products are grotesque, but if you call that beautiful then they are; the one she just finished dangles phone cords like Medusa's hair, gears like jangling medals. Shelves of visors glint under the ceiling fixture; inlaid with chips and broken bits of circuitry, they hum like artifacts from some Byzantium that isn't yet. Two faced Janus masks, their round doll eyes removed; you can wear them either way, male or female, to look in or out.

Gary was staring at them, a strange expression on his face. Like he wanted to throw up.

"Do you think they're good?" I asked, to stop him looking like that.

"Good enough," he said, "if you like dinosaurs."

"I like them. They are strange and wonderful."

"But dinosaurs all the same," he said, his eyes glinting like the mosaic visors. I looked for the source of light on his face but couldn't find it. Maybe he was one of the crazy water men. You hear things, like that's the way they get sometimes; it comes from handling their merchandise too much. Fish-heads, people call them. After the deep ones, the ones that generate their own light.

"Whose water you gettin' now?"

"I never called a water man before today."

"What do you drink?"

"Town water. But I just couldn't do it any more."

"Yeah." It was sad, the way he said it.

"Only cold. For hot we have pots on the stove."

"Uh-huh. Baths down the street at the pool, am I right?"

"Showers, mostly. They don't clean the tubs out too often."

"I guess not."

"I heard your water was the best," I said, threading through the junk to the desk where I keep my checque book. I am a little proud of them, my checques. My buddy and I designed them and he printed them up for me. They're real pretty, with phoenixes and watermelons. I had to clean his kitchen for a week in trade, but it was worth it.

Gary looked interested, his pop-eyes studying the tracery.

"What do I owe you for this fabulous water, Gare?" I asked, punctuating my signature.

He moved his tongue around in his mouth so that his face bulged. A bulge here, a bulge there: his cheek a rolling ball.

"That is some way-out bank you belong to, miss. What did you say it was called?"

"It doesn't have a name. It's my own personal bank. Very secure. These checques are not affected by the stock market."

"And a good thing, too," he nodded, agreeing with me. But he had his doubts. "I tell you what, miss. First delivery's usually free. You see how you like the water, you let me know. But the deposit on the bottles, I got to have that." He glared at me, wanting cash.

I hemmed and hawed, took him on a tour of the premises. Thing was, we had no cash. Well, we had a little, but Deb took it this morning to get her hair done. Half a dozen places in town would rather do your hair on account, and Deb has to pick one that only takes jazz. She can be a prima donna that way. But then, she is the Artiste.

The store is a kind of a hodgepodge. I think she must have a call for the garbage, like a dog whistle; a supersonic whine that only it can hear. Because she cares about it. Garbage is her job; Deb rebirths obsolete appliances, toys, anything thrown away, non-organic. The ones that don't biodegrade, not quickly. It's recycling, only more so; this way they get an extra life on their slow way back to Earth. She makes it into art: sculptures; costumes for Carnival; Heads, mostly. She takes hockey helmets, the domes from those old-style hair dryers, hats, headbands. Anything to go around a head. Hot glue gun, solder, she glues things to them: taken apart washing machines; orphan computers; microwave ovens. The grunts love it. Come February, they buzz in here like flies, picking up a couple of Heads apiece. Grunts have to wear something new every night of Carnival. A good thing, too: jazz. When it first comes in, I just like to do nothing, holding it all morning. It makes my skin happy. Deb doesn't like it; I don't do any work. She comes home, I'm sitting on the floor, playing with the money. She yells, sends me out to the co-op for a year of rice and beans.

Gare and I passed a rack of toys. Thirty years of Christmas, stacked up to the ceiling lights. Between the caved in Atari monitors and the bins full of busted GoBots, almost like an anachronism, was a shoe box of those little plastic domes where the snow is always falling. Gary stopped and picked one out, held it up to the light; a striped yellow fish danced among ferns. Once there had been a thread holding it suspended, but now it floated on its side: gills up, dead. He turned it over and over, like if he just waited long enough, and prayed hard enough, that fish would leap to life.

"It's nice," I said, my feet betraying me, shifting me from one to the other. "I don't think I ever noticed it before."

"Nice? It's amazing! You don't know how long I've been looking for something like this! Look, here's the slot for the battery. It's got a light bulb–this one lights up in the dark!"

"So it does." His enthusiasm made me edgy. I waved the cheque like a slow flag, hoping he'd change his mind about my watermelons.

But he didn't. "Look, miss. I'll take this fish for the deposit. But from now on it's got to be jazz. If you want to keep getting the water."

"Hmm. Maybe town water's not so bad."

He laughed. "It's your funeral."

"I'll give you a call, Gare."

"Sure. If you can find me."

I'd gotten off easy and he was mad. It was just his luck I'd had something he wanted. "Thank you for coming so soon after I called," I said, trying to placate him.

"It's very rare," he grumped. "Collector's material. I can sell it for a week of jazz uptown."

But you won't.

"No problem. I didn't even know we had it."

"No kidding." It was that look again, only in his voice; his hand wrapped around the toy, like he was saving it from something. From me. What did I care. He was almost out the door and then he stopped, staring at the shelves of Heads again. "You make those?"

"I put them together. But my partner, she's the designer."

"She a healer, right?"

"Uh-huh."

"It shows." He nodded at the Heads, looked down at his opened hand, at the fish. He chuckled. It made me look at him, his handsome face, a big grin cutting it in two. You wanted to like him when he grinned. And his hands knocked me out. The brown backs opening to velvet palms, soft and shocking baby pink. Yeesh. I wished I could have hands like that.

He did his other voice, cradling the fish like a baby. "I is going to fix this fish," he crooned. "This is a poor sick fish and needs mending."

The guy was not for real. But his water. "You a fish doctor too, Gare?," I asked, only half sarcastic. He turned on like a light bulb when I said that.

"That's very good, dear. Very, very good." He laughed, a happy laugh from deep down, and for once he didn't look like I made him sick. I was even afraid he wanted to give me a hug; his huge padded arms windmilling towards me like that. I backed away into the warmth; it was freezing, standing there in the opened door. "It's a kind of a side-line, my fish doctoring," he explained. "Like a fiddle. You know what a fiddle is?"

"Yeah, yeah," I said, "Economics 101." I slammed the door while I had a chance. He grinned, turning to cross the road; his feet leaving boat sized holes in the slush. In the middle he stopped to turn and wave again. He was still chuckling when he gunned the van, his big head rolling like it was on bearings. "Pure spring," read the hand-lettered sign on the side. "A drink for sore throats." Weird. Like "a sight for sore eyes."

    ***

Three weeks to go. Deb sleeps at the studio, brings me the new designs in the morning. Flavour of the week is headbands; I've been stringing plastic soldiers onto lengths of ribbon cable. You know the stuff: rows of tiny coloured wires all stuck together, for connecting computers and all. When they're strung each soldier is painted to match a different strand of wire. "Rainbow Warrior," Deb calls 'em.

Two grunts came in this morning and bought Heads. Red Heads, blue Heads; colour is big this year. One also bought a box of old electronic parts, said he wanted to make his own. An arty grunt, yet. He was pale and like his friend wore a grey knee length wool coat. They both looked young. But lately it seems like all the grunts look young: young and spooked.

They made half scared google eyes, told me it was their first time in a place like this: strictly non grunt. Said they worked for banks. Tellers, must be: coats too thin for managers. It almost doesn't rate as a grunt job, being a bank teller. Too servile. Seems like it takes less and less to be a grunt these days. How sad.

"You mean there still is banks?" I asked, doodling on my creative cheque book. I know there is still banks; I just wanted to make them nervous. I'm bad when it comes to young grunts. But jobs. For money. Geez.

***

The secret life of grunts. I do wonder what they think about. They must be on town water. I can't imagine ordering it in and still being a grunt. I can't remember ever even wanting to be a grunt, but I guess grunts want to be grunts. They must. Or else why would they? It's not like you have to be a wage slave. There are other ways.

Another one came in this morning: a creepy older one. He bought my window. It's something I do to relax, when I'm on break from Deb. I climb into the display window and arrange the junk into scenes, make a little Chaos out of the Order. Or is it the other way around? I forget which. Anyway, this time I'd found a plastic Doberman and hot glued its mouth to Barbie's crotch. I know there are worse things on this Earth than a little dog cunnilingus, but even Deb thought it was maybe a little much. The grunt, however, loved it, asked me if I did gift wrap. I did: ripping a strip of red off the velvet curtains left over from Synapses' previous incarnation I tied it around the dog's neck. He loved it, he told me, in that creepy voice; he loved the store and he loved me. "Sure," I said, but I had to get a glass of water right after he left just to get over his face. Maybe that's how it happens to grunts; they get old when the inside faces out too long, when instead of being scared they're scary. And to think I cater to that market. Yeeagh.

***

I used to think all water was the same. It was what you drank for breakfast, had a little coffee to stir in if you were lucky. It was a grunt drink. From Gary I learned otherwise. This morning I brought a quart up to the kitchen where I was working. I heated it up on the stove, and sort of meditated, tried to think how Gary would think it if he was doing the thinking. While I was waiting I amused myself pushing the eyes into a couple of old dolls. I sliced the faces off, attached them one to another with bands of elastic. One male doll, one female, the way you're supposed to do them. A type of Janus. It's not a big seller, but it's lasted; every year we do a few. When the water was warm I put the mask on and drank, using a straw.

I'd pierced the lips for straw holes–grunts won't buy anything they can't drink in. The water went down, warm and wet, and I felt like there were revolving doors inside me, turning, and all of a sudden I could go out the other way. And then I could see the whole deal: how we lived; how we did up our place; what we wore and what we ate: it was all because of drinking the town water. And this thing about getting your own water, it really worked. I could see how tacky it was: Synapses, Deb's and my life. A cheesy, no-class deal, except for some of the Heads. Like the Janus Head. It was clean, a nice idea made flesh. I kept it on, poking around the place, looking out the eyes of Gary's water. It was fun. I saw things I hadn't seen before, like which things fit together and how come. I poked around in shoe boxes all afternoon, looking at junk.

Every day they bring more in. I wonder where it all comes from. Junk out of plastic, junk out of metal. They don't make so much junk as they used to, but boy, when they did, was it ever a going concern. It must have employed thousands of people, the junk industry. I wonder where they got the raw materials from. I mean, what is that cheap-o plastic made of, anyway? What natural substance has been humiliated in its service? I kind of got lost in the beauty of it, the beautiful ugliness of the cheap plastic objects I was handling. It occurred to me then they were beautiful precisely because they were ugly, and I even know a few people like that. And the more my thoughts headed off in that direction the gladder I became I work for Deb. Because, you know, I used to feel sorry for them. We'd be shopping for clothes at Thrift Villa or wherever, and there'd be shelves full of broken down toasters and waffle irons, and I'd think how nobody cared about them, not even my Mom. Everyone always wanting the new one: clean ones, without any scratches or deformities, in good working order and with high IQ's. That is why I love Deb so much. She was the first person to see that all that old stuff wanted to still be used; it wanted so badly to have a purpose for us. So Deb thought and thought of how to use it, and finally she came up with the whole style of wearing garbage to Carnival, and now everyone does it, us and all the grunts.

***

Things have been different lately, I don't know why. Funny thoughts come to me while I work. That we are like fish in an aquarium, looking out at the world. I think it's since Gary came that it's been different. I never did any of that computing but my buddy Danny, the one who does the cheques, he told me it is like that. Programming. It is like going into inner space. And I think maybe Gary's water is like that too, like going into space. To think I never knew. No wonder he was looking at me like that.

***

Two weeks. Carnival soon. I've started a new window. I work on it during breaks. TV sets done up like aquariums. Somehow they look the same: a clear glass box. I have a milk crate full of plastic fish; I string them from the inside of the TVs so they look like they're swimming. Take the picture tubes out, of course. And one real aquarium. A glass fish bowl I found upstairs that fits perfectly into one of the smaller TVs. I went down to the store and bought live fish for it. I paid for them with some of the grunt money. The dog grunt money, to be precise. I lied to Deb, told her Danny gave them to me, that I washed his floors for him. She doesn't like me doing anything that costs money. Also she doesn't understand I have to make my own art sometimes. The windows. That's my art. That and the thoughts, the weird water ones.

***

Out of water. Once you get the new water, it's hard to go back to the old. I haven't thought so much in years. Even Deb likes me better, gives me time off in the afternoons to work on the window. It's very beautiful, now, almost finished. I wonder how I ever did dogs and dolls. I could never go back to that now. Phoned Gary but there was no answer. Shit. Town water sucks.

***

Don't forget to dream. To bring in the new world. Otherwise the old one just keeps rolling on. Death as predecessor to rebirth. The seed, sleeping in the earth. The purpose of winter. Subtle changes taking place, deep in the darkness underground. Winter, Carnival, bringing back the sun. New windows. Fish televisions? But what is the death? The underworld. Being fish. What will we be, when we're not fish?

***

First day of Carnival. The grunts pour into the street, displaying their wares. Who will buy, and who will be bought? The one time of year they get to ease up. Bread and circus. For two weeks they live what is ours the whole year through. I felt so still, so empty inside. Deb was out, being photographed for something. I sat in the window, watching the grunts parading, wearing their garbage regalia. They were beautiful: moving in slow motion, with dream smiles on their faces. They looked happy. I recognized some of their Heads as ones we'd done. They smiled and waved at me, sitting among my fish TVs. Who is looking in and who is looking out? It is like the Janus mask. Tomorrow I will wear it.

    ***

I feel so still. In Carnival they act it out, the death and rebirth. But this year it's like it's real: Janus eyes in the back of my head. Gary came. He grinned and gesticulated, stamping his feet on the other side of the glass. He waved his hands. I wanted to see it, his beautiful skin, but he was wearing mitts. He brought the water. He carried it into the window where I was sitting, and we each had some. It was cool and clean and good, running down our throats in the cold morning. When we weren't thirsty any more he made me come outside, showed me how Synapses' window was like a television too, or an aquarium, and I the fish in it. I knew where there was a big box of grease crayons in the back, and we drew it onto the glass: the outline of the screen and the control panel. I even found a fish costume in a drawer of stuff Deb did before there were Heads.

***

He sat beside me for a long time, and we looked out the window, part of the display. A big quiet black man and a thin white girl dressed up as a fish. The Carnival faces passed us, a white dressed throng, wearing Heads made of all their old stuff, and I was content as I've ever been. Finally understanding it, the meaning of Carnival. The old flesh dying to the new. They passed with the skeleton then, an effigy held high above their heads.

"Whose death is it this time, Gare?" I asked.

He put his big mitten out, covering my knee. "It is the death of Death."

"And the birth of Life?"

"Yes."

"That's what I thought. I'm glad I'm here to see this one."

"It is an interesting time."

He rose stiffly in his great padded knees, wearing a parka and thick quilted pants like always.

"I will be going then."

"I'm glad I know you, Gary."

"I, too. I will be coming by from time to time, to see how you are doing."

"Goodbye, Gary, goodbye."

***

Roses. It will be the next window. Flowers will bloom out of all the televisions there are. In the meantime it snows. Soft white snow falling like it does in a plastic bubble of fish, its string re-paired. It sits on top of one of the televisions, where Gary left it for me to discover. Its light bulb glows softly in the darkening day.

The End

CHRIS BIRD

Chris Bird *is a Londoner inspired by the energy and history of this great city. He worked in Istanbul for Time Out magazine and has been creating his own zines for years. He is influenced by music such as The Stooges and The Fall and writers such as Jean Rhys and William Burroughs.*

THE SEA BOOKS
by Chris Bird

They washed up on the shore in the early spring morning unseen and uninvited. At first there were only four or five moving on the brisk waves. Riding the white water they landed on the level brown sand like massive shells from the ocean floor. Then each day the numbers increased, left in clusters on the sand by the ebb and flow of the sea. Soon people came from the nearby village to see.

The books came every day, sometimes embedded with starfish and seahorses or shells and glossy seas tones and pebbles dredged up by the tide. The words, blurred by the sea often slipped out of the hard covers and drifted across the sea's surface into rock pools spelling out intricate new meanings.

The fishermen dragged the increasing piles of books in from the sea and stacked them along the beach and the rocks. The village priest came to inspect them for sacrilegious content but went away disappointed when he found none. A retired general dug a shallow trench near the books under a flapping national flag. However he couldn't decide on any further military response. He persuaded two volunteers to stand sentry on the beach head to monitor the incursions.

Local politicians made committed speeches both in favour and against the crowding piles of books. As the numbers increased further the villagers noticed that the covers of the books were etched with strange symbols such as stars, moon crescents, sea snakes, spiders, keys, domes, ladders and random numbers and letters. When they opened the individual books the words poured from the pages and drained away before their eyes. One inventive villager requisitioned a great pile of the books and made a bonfire of them. He and his children watched the crackling words rise on the flames floating amongst white ash up into the night sky.

But as the numbers continued to increase the night grew gradually darker. The villagers noticed that there were far fewer stars in the sky each night. The night sky became an empty blackness over the thatched roofs of the village where once there had been shimmering constellations. Divisions between the villagers as to how best to respond to the gathering deluge of books created hither to unknown social tension in the village. A number of new political parties were soon formed.

Soon two principal factions solidified. One group argued that the books should be dumped into an open pit and then burnt using gasoline. Their opponents wanted to construct an enormous monument in adoration of the sea's unsolicited gift.

The gradual loss of the stars intensified the crisis. One faction, in an attempt to blame their opposition for the loss of the stars wore large star shaped emblems as masks in night time rallies beside the shore. Another faction draped themselves with symbolic wooden flames painted orange and gold. The small community took to segregating themselves on either side of a village dividing line known as the 'Sea Word Wall'.

Then as the crisis smoldered on the books on the shore began to rot. A great stench rose up from them and a slimy grey green moss began to crawl over them forming hill like mounds on the beach.

The 'New Sea Hills', as they became known, swarmed with flies and mosquitoes and the stench swayed over the entire village. A group of young men rolled a stone boulder down the cliff to break up the nauseous mounds of books. Another gang shot fireworks down at the slimy mass to burn it away.

Crabs and sea insects burrowed into the decomposing words to build new homes. Gulls and herons nested on the green mounds. The sea began to wash over the massive hills as if trying to reclaim it.

Local politicians tried to get control of the crisis by inserting national flags and party banners into the mounds. This, they argued, would prevent them from being annexed by unscrupulous foreign powers. The village priest hurriedly added crucifixes and icons and expressed hopes of an ornamental bell tower on the highest mound. An artist described his aim to re colour the green mass blue as a symbolic tribute to the book's original source. Certain extremists were held responsible for a small explosion on one of the mossy peaks.

But the plans of the disparate groups were soon overshadowed as first one child and then another fell seriously ill. The illness spread rapidly from family to family. The children fell ill with a flu like virus which quickly became more serious. Within a few days the children fell into a deep sleep which continued uninterrupted day after day. Later strange boils grew on the children's fingertips and tongues. The boils only grew on these particular points. The village doctor was bemused and could find no cure. Over seventy children fell ill. All slept soundlessly while their fingertips and tongues throbbed red. Mothers kept each other awake in the early hours with their tears and sobbing.

Fishermen hauled a wide net over part of the mass and tried to drag it back into the sea with a flotilla of fishing boats. But their attempt came to nothing. The books could not be shifted. Spring soon turned to summer and the rotting stench of the books intensified. Flies swarmed incessantly over the putrid mounds.

There seemed to be no end to the villagers suffering. At night as they decomposed distorted echoes of words moaned and wailed out across the village's thatched rooftops. No one could ignore the strange sounds and no one could sleep through the long summer nights. One frail old man lost his senses and leapt from a cliff top into the mounds where crutches and all he sank slowly from view. The sea gulls called and sang in ecstatic loops of flight over the 'New Sea Hills', peeling away to dive at isolated crabs amongst the decaying words. The sea rolled back and forth and the long summer days were tainted by the acrid smell of the books. Crabs grew fat on the digest of words, hornets and mosquitoes saturated the moss with countless eggs.

But the news of the village children was not good. As the fingertips and tongues reddened further single words grew from the blemishes and wounds. Their injuries spelt out new cryptic sentences.

No boats left in the early morning to fish. The fishing nets were overrun and clogged with decaying words. The word mass gradually began to seep over the cliff tops and spread along the narrow village streets. Families had to move to higher ground around the village church.

The children passed away one by one and were laid in the cemetery ground. Wrapped in cotton shrouds their injuries poured open with contrived obscenities and blasphemies. From their graves strange purple flowers grew, each petal of which contained a word or message.

The priest himself could take no more and was found dangling from a noose from the highest church beam in a mossy rope he had made from the sea hills. The local militia having peppered the mounds with cannon balls and grenades to no avail mutinied in despair and ran in ragged uniforms into the sea.

The disease then spread from child to mother and then to father. Wreaths, lilies and poppies adorned the silent doorways of the village houses. Superstition led to the building of a huge straw man which was torched and then pushed from a cliff top down onto the mass of words. The straw man burnt in gold and amber flames on the mass of words.

Then as the morning sun glowed over the half empty village the mass began to shift and stir. Gradually the mass of words began to harden. A week later it had solidified even further. The mossy appearance gave way to a new stone like hardness. A month passed by and slowly cracks and splits appeared on the surface of the stony word hills. The cracks only appeared at night and only on nights when the moon glowed strongly onto the beach.

One night a few villagers crawled to the edge of a cliff top and with binoculars and telescopes observed the cracks and openings widening noticeably. For another week the mass crackled and shifted, tearing here and there in jagged moonlit openings.

Then one night, watched by a small group of fishermen, the mass split into two enormous boulders, one of which crashed into the rough night sea. The two huge boulders began to crack and groan. Slowly new cracks opened up on the surfaces of the two boulders. Through the moonlit night these cracks opened further and further until suddenly the two boulders simultaneously split apart. From inside stepped two gigantic figures, naked and covered with seaweed and shells. The figures slowly stood on the sand, stretching and yawning. Their skin was almost transparent in the silvery moonlight.

Together the giant man and woman walked out toward the sea. Their bodies shone and beneath the pale surface of their skin crawling one over the other were thousands upon thousands of words, linking and splitting, fusing and diverging in endless shifting patterns shimmering in the summer moonlight.

CHRIS BIRD

Ben Beck has lived in London for most of his life. He is author of the website on Anarchism and Science Fiction, http://benbeck.co.uk/anarchysf/main.htm. Through his interest in family history he is proud to have learnt that his great-grandfather was a personal friend of both Peter Kropotkin and William Morris.

H.G. WELLS AND ANARCHISM
by Ben Beck

Wells—arguably the grandfather of modern science fiction—was a political dabbler who never understood the need for harmonizing ends and means. Anarchism as a future dream he found attractive, but in the contemporary world he directed his activities to the globalization of the state.

Wells's earliest reference to anarchism in his fiction, is in his 1894 story 'The Stolen Bacillus'', in which an anarchist steals a tube of what he believes to be cholera bacillus but is actually a bacterium which makes monkeys come out in blue patches. It is light humour, but very much at the expense of the anarchist, whose portrayal is a classic caricature: he is "slender", "pale-faced" and "morbid", with a "limp white hand", his undiscriminating motive being apparently no more than the revenge of the little man against society. In "The Diamond Maker" (1895), the inventor of a process for the manufacture of diamonds finds it more a liability than an asset: he is taken for an anarchist, and before long the evening papers describe his den as "the Kentish-Town Bomb Factory".

The Time Machine (1895), *The War of the Worlds* (1898), *The First Men in the Moon* (1901), and *The War in the Air* (1908) have no specific anarchist interest, though they have been considered, purely as novels, by anarchist critics including Herbert Read, George Woodcock, and Michael Moorcock.

In 1896 Wells published *The Island of Dr Moreau*: Moreau, a notorious vivisector, sets up his lab on a South Pacific island and attempts to surgically construct humans from animals; as they revert they turn upon and kill Moreau and his collaborator, only the castaway narrator escaping. This work had some interest for George Woodcock, who not only drew attention to similarities between this novel and Frankenstein, but also viewed it as a precursor of the great dystopian novels of the twentieth century. The "significant and horrible thing in this book," he says, "is not the physical vivisection by which animals are turned into the semblances of men, but the psychological conditioning by which their minds are made to work in the kind of mass pattern required by the ruler."

BLAIR GAUNTT

In *The Invisible Man* (1897) a scientist discovers the secret of invisibility, but finds it irreversible; getting increasingly desperate he wreaks havoc in a country town, and is eventually killed. At one point Griffin, the scientist, had been taken by a villager for "an Anarchist in disguise, preparing explosives". Anarchist critics, like others, have seen this work as "perhaps symbolic of science run amok for lack of responsibility."

A Modern Utopia (1905) is exactly that—Wells's vision of a technologically-developed world state, ruled by an enlightened cast, the 'Samurai'. It is, in his view, a realistic alternative to the too-perfect Nowhere of William Morris. Predictably, anarchist writers have found it unattractive: "as ethical and disciplinarian as Plato" (Ethel Mannin); "Wells's conception of freedom turns out to be a very narrow one" (Marie-Louise Berneri). Woodcock found Wells's proposal for a samurai elite "disturbing". For all that, this is easily the best-informed modern utopia, a landmark of utopian literature, and worth reading on that ground, if not for its political sympathies.

In *The Future in America* (1906) Wells recounts the tale of William MacQueen, an anarchist who in 1902 received a five-year sentence for his involvement in the Paterson weaver's strike, though he had done no more than speak. Wells met MacQueen while in the USA, and was quite taken with him, finding him "much my sort of man". MacQueen, a Tolstoyan, had declined to speak on the same platform as Emma Goldman, whom Wells describes as "a mischievous and violent lady anarchist".

His *Socialism and the Family* (1906) was reviewed in the English anarchist newspaper Freedom in 1907, the reviewer regretfully concluding that "in Mr Wells we have one more apostle of the State". The conclusion was regretted because there is a notable passage in this book in which Wells speaks of anarchy as an ideal:

"When one comes to dreams, when one tries to imagine one's finest sort of people, one must surely imagine them too fine for control and prohibitions, doing right by a sort of inner impulse, 'above the Law.' One's dreamland perfection is Anarchy—just as no one would imagine a policeman (or for the matter of that a drain-pipe) in Heaven. But come down to earth, to men the descendants of apes, to men competing to live, and passionately jealous and energetic, and for the highways and market-places of life at any rate, one asks for law and convention. In Heaven or any Perfection there will be no Socialism, communism, anarchism, universal love and universal service. It is in the workaday world of limited and egotistical souls that Socialism has its place. All men who dream at all of noble things are Anarchists in their dreams..."

From the same year (1906) is Wells's scientific romance *In the Days of the Comet*: tortured romance prior to the Earth being brushed by a comet's tail is followed by a happy foursome after the event; the whole world is magically transformed. In *Socialism and the Family* Wells wrote of this novel that he had been "forced by the logic of his premises and even against his first intention to present not a Socialist State but a glorious anarchism as the outcome of that rejuvenescence of the world." If so, it is an anarchism more curious than glorious, for the polity is in fact a world state, with written laws.

In *New Worlds for Old* (1909), subtitled *A Plain Account of Modern Socialism,* Wells distinguishes two kinds of anarchism. One is the perfect ideal described above, which he finds exemplified in the utopias of Morris and W.H. Hudson; again, however, he emphasizes that the way to reach it is "through education and discipline and law". The other is that of the historical anarchist movement, which he absolutely rejects; for him this anarchism is "as it were a final perversion of the Socialist stream, a last meandering of Socialist thought, released from vitalizing association with an active creative experience. Anarchism comes when the Socialist repudiation of property is dropped into the circles of thought of men habitually ruled and habitually irresponsible Anarchism, with its knife and bomb, is a miscarriage of Socialism, an acephalous birth from that fruitful mother."

In *The Sleeper Awakes* (1910—first published in 1899 as *When the Sleeper Wakes*) Graham, the Sleeper, wakes up after 200+ years of suspended animation to find himself master of the world and a King Arthur figure for the downtrodden masses. Ostrog successfully stages a coup d'état in his name, but when he in turn proved a tyrant Graham sides alone with the masses; premature rebellion fails, however, and Graham is killed in the world's first ever aerial dogfight. Woodcock found the work "terrifyingly negative", "a prison-vision of the soulless economic and political tyranny that seems to him one possible conclusion of the industrial revolution". Though a powerful vision, it is marred for present-day readers by Graham only being really roused to activity by the prospect of black African forces being used to crush discontent ("'White men must be mastered by white men'", Graham says). Wells correctly shows the inevitability of Ostrog's corrupt assumption of power, but fails to explain why Graham should be expected to be any different—he wants to side with Graham, but you can't help feeling he actually rather admires Ostrog.

His 1911 novel *The New Machiavelli*—not SF—refers to the Chicago anarchists, has a minor character with anarchistic leanings, and was reviewed in Goldman's Mother Earth: "Wells is always at his best when the politician in him is silenced and the artist allowed to speak." In his 1896 review of William Morris's The Well at the World's End Wells had recalled discussions at Kelmscott House in the 1880s in which the Chicago anarchists were much featured.

The World Set Free (1914) is an important early prediction of nuclear war, but regrettably tedious to read.

Men Like Gods (1923) is Wells's second utopia, set on a parallel Earth. Government as such withered away about 1000 years before, its place being taken by some discrete coordination of functions coupled with a perfected education: young Utopians are inculcated with the "Five Principles of Liberty, without which civilization is impossible", these being the Principles of Privacy, Free Movement, Unlimited Knowledge, "that Lying is the Blackest Crime", and free discussion and criticism. One of the earthlings transported as observers to the parallel Utopia finds society there to be a "peculiar form of Anarchism", but in view of the character's portrayed ignorance this is not Wells's view, unless you stress the "peculiar". George Woodcock touched on this work on several occasions, describing it as "a kind of high-class celestial suburbia of appalling uniformity", but also as "the Godwinian society" brought into line with the speculations of Edwardian scientists. Later he drew attention to Wells's decision to use a parallel world treatment, rather than a straight future setting; this was "his essential pessimism"—Utopia can't really be part of our future. Marie-Louise Berneri, in her *Journey Through Utopia*, regarded *Men Like Gods* as "*Wells's News from Nowhere*, a Nowhere which would have been too scientific and streamlined for Morris's taste, but which gets rid of much of the bureaucracy, coercion and moral compulsion that pervade *A Modern Utopia*." My own feeling is that it is still the same utopia, but with the authoritarianism better concealed.

His realist novel *The World of William Clissold* (1926) mentions Godwin and Proudhon, and was reviewed in Freedom, whose reviewer appreciated the work as "provocative".

In *Mr Blettsworthy on Rampole Island* (1928) Blettsworthy spends several years on an island of cannibals, where megatheria still live—except that it all turns out to be his own psychotic delusions. Perhaps underrated as a work of SF, it is of considerable interest here for a few pages towards the end, in which the trial and judicial murder of Sacco and Vanzetti play a prominent role. Blettsworthy, recovering from his delusion that he is on an island of savages, suffers a relapse on the night of their execution. Clearly speaking for Wells himself, he explains that he is "one of that considerable number of people who are compelled to think these men were innocent of the crime for which they suffered, that they were tried with prejudice and upon a wrong charge and that the revision of their sentence was one of those issues that test the moral and intellectual values of a great community". In his renewed fantasy Sacco and Vanzetti are transformed into missionaries to the benighted Rampole Island, and all the islanders symbolically share in the guilt of their executioners by partaking sacramentally of their flesh.

The Shape of Things to Come (1933), though well-known (probably more for its filmed version as *Things to Come*), is surely one of Wells's worst SF works, dreary to the point of unreadability. It is supposedly the history, as written from 2105, of the preceding two centuries, covering the period of the triumph of the world state. Though at one point the future historian casts a relatively sympathetic eye on the anarchist outrages of the nineteenth century, since behind them, "even though vague, exaggerated and distorted, was the hope of a new world order", the overall tone is of unconcealed admiration for authoritarianism: the Italian Fascists and the Russian Community Party are described as a "partial but very real advance on democratic institutions", and "Fascism indeed was not an altogether bad thing..." At the conclusion of the book, quite incredibly, the World Council abdicates; this asks too much of the reader's credulity, so in no way mitigates the predominant adulation of power.

In *The Open Conspiracy* (1930) he took issue with Proudhon's assertion that property is robbery, finding it rather "the protection of things against promiscuous and mainly wasteful use". He had taken similar exception to Proudhon in Socialism and the Family, and did so again in two works of 1934. In *The Work, Wealth and Happiness of Mankind* he considers anarchism as the "next stage to representative democracy"; he also rightly identifies it as the logical conclusion to the premises of pacifism. In his Experiment in Autobiography he acknowledges Godwin and Shelley as influences on his own beliefs regarding women, love, and marriage. Rather extraordinarily, he also derides William Morris for his sympathy with the Haymarket Martyrs.

Star-Begotten: A Biological Fantasia (1937) is a very slight late work speculating on the possibility of Martians tampering with evolution on Earth. At one point there is some speculation on a future in which the Martian-influenced Homo superior will refuse to fight wars, manufacture armaments, and obey dictators, in which tyrannicide is the norm. This vision is specifically likened to anarchism, which is in this way shown in a favourable light, as Wells concludes that the Martian influence should be welcomed.

In the 1940s, Wells was once persuaded to write a piece of prose fiction for George Woodcock's *NOW* magazine. The work, described by Woodcock as "sadly bumbling", was rejected.

Davi Barker was born in California and during childhood travels he was struck by the wonders of nature -- a lightning storm over a primordial desert in Arabia, or the cherry blossom petals sprinkling down on the floating markets in Thailand. He spent his adolescence as an outsider, but recently is realizing alienation is not uniqueness, but a universal similarity that crosses all cultures and religions, caused by our separation from our true self and our separation from nature. Davi's website is http://muslimagorist.com/

SOMALIA 2030: ALL THE KING'S MEN

by Davi Barker

An old man's hands trembled as he wet his daughter's forehead with a damp rag. All around them glass was breaking and stone was crumbling as the city was bombarded by cannon fire from war ships in the harbor. Her contractions were now eight minutes apart and she lay on a straw bed. Suddenly a young man ran in shouting, "Qadi Jilani! The clans have assembled to defend the port. You are the elder. They're waiting for your ruling."

"No!" Insisted the old man. "The port has been a place of peace between the clans for a decade. We will not sacrifice that so easily. I will go to the Ethiopian King, and seek a diplomatic resolution. I must go to the port alone."

The woman grabbed Jilani's arm, her body convulsing. "You're not leaving me here!"

Another blast tore through a neighboring cottage. The walls shook as books flew from the shelves. Dust billowed.

Jilani replied, "No Amina. Not here." He turned to the boy. "You must gather the defenseless and flea to the mountains." The boy froze. "Go now! See that Amina is safe!"

***

Jilani was the elder judge of the Pwnt clan, which was the dominant clan of Mogadishu. The Pwnt, and Jilani specifically, were instrumental in negotiating and preserving the peace that Mogadishu had enjoyed since the United Nations was abolished. The UN had promised financial aid to whichever Warlord could convincingly claim to be the elected leader of Somalia, but the Somali people had never been impressed with democracy. The only way to impose it on them was by force, and so the UN slush fund only incentivized violence among the impressionable young. But a few elders remembered the Somali people's pre-colonial customary law, which was practiced before democracy had ever failed in their lands. After 10 years of the social software indigenous to their nation they had established a modest prosperity in the traditional way, by the sweat of their brow.

The moral force commanded by Jilani's reputation was known throughout the Horn of Africa. So, when Jilani ordered the assembled clans of Somalia to stand down they listened. And when he approached the Ethiopian infantry alone and unarmed, even they recognized him, and he was granted a quorum with the field marshal who called himself, "King."

***

Jilani was brought behind a line of assault vehicles to a mobile command center. It had the look of a large recreational vehicle, complete with gun ports and heavy armor. Inside King Abraha sat in a large command chair surrounded by multiple large control screens giving him seamless communication with the units in the field.

It was with hubris that Abraha ordered the Ethiopian people to bow before him. But it was the custom of the Somali people never to bow before anyone. Needless to say that custom did not ingratiate Jilani to King Abraha.

"If it isn't the renowned Qadi Jilani. Always faithful to the old customs I see." Abraha was dressed in the likeness of a British military commander, with an orange beret and a lapel full of pins describing honors he'd awarded himself.

"They have served us well enough." Jilani answered.

"You are living in the past, old friend. You are ignoring the march of progress. Of democracy and industry."Abraha swelled with pride.

Jilani leaned on the spiraled driftwood he used as a walking stick, "You call this progress? You have abandoned the law of your people."

"I AM THE LAW OF MY PEOPLE!" Abraha bristled. "Enough of this… I suppose you have come to present the terms of your surrender?"

"Quite the opposite. I have come to demand restitution."

"Demand?" Abraha scoffed. "What sort of restitution?"

"My family's cottage was damaged by your bombardments, and our herds were disbursed. I'd like them replaced."

"Goats!?" Abraha laughed.

"Camels." Jilani retorted in precisely the same tone.

"I am here to destroy your port and the great Qadi Jilani only cares about some camels?"

Jilani continued, revealing nothing. "I am the master of the herd, not the master of the port." He paused. "So, you have not come to conquer?"

"This plot of dirt? Certainly not! My only aim is to demolish the port of Mogadishu. Did you know I have built a magnificent port in Djibouti? It is state of the art, with all the modern conveniences, and I have ordered my people to go there. But that order was ignored!" The King's wrath began to swell in his face. "Still Mogadishu is the center of trade. Why?!"

Jilani calmly replied, "Perhaps peace is good for business."

"No!" Abraha slammed his fist on the table. "Peace is good for business. War is good for business. I'll tell you why they come here! You have created a haven for black market criminals... pirates and terrorists! And by harboring Ethiopian ships in defiance of Ethiopian law you steal commerce that rightfully belongs to us. Taxes that rightfully belong to me!"

Jilani could not mask a look of incredulity, but did not interrupt.

"But I am a righteous king. I have not come here to demand restitution for the taxes you have stolen from me. I do not even wish to fight you. I will settle for the demolition of the port. If you do not resist, I will even replace your camels. But if you resist, you will be crushed by a larger and better equipped army than all the clans of Mogadishu put together. I'll give you 48 hours."

***

Jilani returned to the assembled clans of Mogadishu and informed them of the kings demands. He advised that the people should join him and flee into the mountains for safety, but one from his own clan voiced his adamant disagreement. Ababil was a younger man, an agriculturalist, who lead those from the Pwnt clan who wanted war. The other clans were split. Some fled, others stayed to fight, and despite the great disparity in arms they fought valiantly. They charged Abraha's army from the west and in a day of glorious battle two armies were destroyed, both the Ethiopians and the Somalis, leaving no aggressors left in Mogadishu.

Amina delivered a baby boy, but died in childbirth. Jilani took charge of the child, swore to keep him safe from aggression, and named him Hakim.

BLAIR GAUNTT

Chapter Two: The Dark Hour

It was an impossibly quiet night. Away from city lights, on moonless nights, the stars appear more brilliant than most people have ever seen. But to the ancients the night sky was a tapestry of signs.

"The dark hour" a voice pierced the cool air.

"What is the dark hour?" asked another, and then the night returned to reverent silence.

A pause.

"It is the darkest part of the night. Before dawn is when it happens. Soon the false dawn will appear."

"What is the false dawn?"

Another silence.

"Pay attention."

The two looked into the darkness.

In the East a vertical beam of white light extended upward from the horizon across the arc of the sky. As it grew it was followed by a cold milky haze.

"The false dawn is brightest near the autumn equinox. But there's no rosy hue like the true dawn, just a pale grey. There is a special blessing in the hours before the true dawn. A tranquility in the air. A spiritual traveler should always wake before the sun, when our minds and bodies are refreshed. It is a time of reflection and rumination before the business of the day clouds our minds."

"So what should we be reflecting on?"

"Sit child, I will tell you the story of The Herdsman and the Lion."

A long long time ago our clan convened an assembly of our elders to appoint a sultan who was granted executive powers. And so they chose a man named Assad the Lion who was both a ferocious warrior and a wise jurist. He was known for his courage, and wit. But he quickly abandoned the Law and began legislating new decrees our ancestors had never seen.

Sultan Assad ordered that for every meal he would eat only the bone marrow of young goats, which is the creamiest most delicious part of the animal. He said that the rich protein would keep him strong, both in body and mind, and was sure that the clan would recognize the value of his strong leadership. But after feeding the Sultan this way for several days the clansmen began to worry. To satisfy the Sultan's appetite they had to slaughter ten goats every day, and their herds were rapidly dwindling.

One day a herdsman came to the Sultan to plead with him that if he didn't change the rate of his consumption they will have slaughtered every goat in every herd within three months. Assad the Lion called him forward and in an act of cold calculation he cut out the herdsman's tongue. The herdsman screamed as blood poured from his mouth, but no one dared to come to his aid. That night the Sultan ate the tongue with his evening meal.

But it was too late. The people had heard the warning of the herdsman and knew the direness of their situation. The clan elders convened a second assembly, this time in secret, to discuss their predicament.

The elders thought a coup was in order, and that it was time to plot the murder of the Sultan. They argued that if they all joined together they could overpower Assad the Lion. But the herdsman objected (in writing of course). He argued that if they overthrew the Sultan by violent means the result would only be the rise of another tyrant. So, he devised a different plan.

Bone marrow is very fatty. So, for one month they would gradually increase the Sultan's portions. Meanwhile, the rest of the clan would perform the fast of King David, only eating every other day, to discipline their appetites. After a month Assad had become accustomed to meals nearly twice as large, and had gained considerable weight, while the rest of the clan had become lean and efficient, accustomed to hunger.

Then one day the herdsman returned to the Sultan, but since he could not speak he brought a written declaration. It was a manifesto of reform which he presented to Assad. It described the discontentment of his clansmen, and served him an ultimatum. The declaration was signed by every herdsman, every farmer and every baker in the clan pledging to slaughter not one beast, harvest not one crop and bake not one loaf until he peacefully and voluntarily relinquished his appointment. There would be no more bone marrow.

Enraged, the Sultan tore the document to shreds declaring that the clan could not survive without him. He drew a billao dagger and lunged at the herdsman, but he was made clumsy by his obesity and the herdsman easily dodged. The Sultan fell flat on his belly and the assembled crowd laughed, humiliating him in his own court.

The next day the Sultan went barging into people's homes looking for food, but he found none. On the second day he went to the orchards to steal fruit but he found people ready to defend their property, and himself in no condition to fight. On the third day he marched out into the grazing pastures to slaughter a goat himself, but he was so fat from marrow and weak from hunger that he couldn't catch one. The chase left him exhausted, wheezing in the dirt.

The herdsman approached him in the field, but the Sultan was too weak to get up. He laid on the ground gasping for air as the herdsman stood over him without speaking. Once he caught his breath Assad the Lion cried out, "I submit. I submit. I submit!" and began weeping. The herdsman bent forward and took Assad's head in his hands. With one hand he pet his hair and with the other he fed him a fist full of raw oats, as he did to sooth a frightened animal.

Assad became known from then on as Assad the Lamb, and lived out his life in humiliated obscurity. He was never trusted to serve as a jurist for the clan ever again. His only role was to be a servant to the herdsman in restitution for the injury. The herdsman became one of our clan's wisest and most celebrated jurists, and Assad was charged with reading his written statements. And the elders resolved to never appoint another Sultan.

There was a green flash and then twilight. The sky turned gray and then blue. The stars faded. Like a wave, a roar swept over the valley. Birds began to sing. The grass and trees came to life with a soft rustle. And there was no more silence.

Faces became discernible again. Young Hakim and his grand-father Jilani, the elder jurist of their clan, sat around the coals and ashes of last night's fire. Paying attention.

The child looked puzzled. "I don't understand. Why didn't they just overpower Assad at the beginning? They wouldn't have lost all those goats."

Jilani stroked his beard. "It is part of the natural Law that the ends will always contain their means. What made Assad a tyrant was that he deviated from the natural way, or most precisely the elders did by appointing him. You cannot return to the natural way by unnatural means. If they had resolved to murder him their result would contain violence. Without addressing the original deviation the elders they would have only replaced him with a new sultan, likely whoever lead the party that killed him. And there's no telling how many lives would have been lost, or how many goats a new tyrant would demand. Not to mention, if they had killed Assad he would not have been alive to offer restitution."

"I think I understand. But how do you know what the natural way is?"

"That's a question for another night. I have affairs to attend to." Jilani stood up, using a piece of spiraled drift wood as a cane. "Stay here as long as you like. Think a lot. The sunrise will be soon. It will be beautiful. The next time we meet we will discuss the Law."

Jilani began walking down the mountain, leaving Hakim alone with his thoughts.

The Aftermath

The first light of dawn these days is not white, but amber, when the sun hangs in the penumbra between the horizon and the haze left from the Great Fire.

The morning poured through a broken window, between gimcracks and gadgets, and found the sleeping face of young Hakim. As he stirred, he reached over to his night stand to activate an electric generator.

A few coughs and whirls and the room sprang to life. Lights flashed and flickered, screens ignited and the haunting chords of Auslander blasted at full volume. Hakim rolled out of bed into a pile of clothes and emerged in ragged jeans and a "DISOBEY" t-shirt. He walked down an empty hallway past dusty bedrooms to the kitchen, where he boiled water for tea and prepared a simple breakfast of cornmeal porridge, sweet bread, and sesame oil.

It was important to conserve the generator, as petrol was becoming scarce. Hakim generally allowed only an hour for his mobile devices to charge. While he waited, he perused the news of the day. Locally, the weather was clear and the cease-fire had held through the night, which was good for business. Globally, governments continued to collapse in a heap of paper under the weight of their own tedious make-work bureaucracies. The headlines announced that this week Uganda had joined the ranks of the stateless, while the government of New Zealand had followed the precedent led by America and resolved its debt crisis by auctioning off most of its territory to sovereign business franchises, in this case a number of competing pastoral farming and agricultural companies. Hakim was pleased to see that the expected result was a drop in global food prices, but the cost of petrol continued to rise as government subsidies dried up. Yesterday it had spiked 10,000 Kred a barrel.

Hakim was too young to have ever lived under a State. It simply wasn't the custom of the Somali people. To him it was utterly alien to divide society into two classes of rulers and the ruled, and it seemed to him that the only purpose of government was to harass people and eat out their substance.

He finished his breakfast, freshened up, and powered down the generator. No sense leaving it running all day. In his neighborhood, streets were so run down, vehicles couldn't navigate them—not that many people drove anymore. His only neighbors lived in disheveled housing developments defended by private security. Herds of goats grazed grasses that punctuated the concrete guarded by shepherds armed with Kalashnikovs. Vegetable gardens sprang up in any gated lot that had soil. The public rail no longer ran. Public power and water were gone too. Almost all commerce took place near the port, but to get there, he had to walk three full kilometers to reach the private roads.

New Mogadishu

Once you get within ten kilometers of the port, you have a choice. The local taxi and bus drivers had formed Jidkha Lines, which privately repaired the public roads. Local drivers knew the best routes, and you could negotiate a good price to get anywhere in the city, especially if you don't mind ride-sharing. In addition,

Breezeways, a foreign company, had invested in constructing and maintaining a higher quality network of privately owned expressways. The catch was that to gain access to the expressways you had to rent an electric vehicle from their fleet, but those weren't rugged enough for most of the public roads. They were designed for smoother rides.

Hakim had determined that the most cost-effective solution for him was to rent a bicycle from any one of the local shops, because neither company objected to pedestrians and bicyclists using their roads, and it meant his transportation expenses were not subject to the fluctuating price of petrol. In addition, by clipping a drag condenser to the rear wheel, he could generate electricity to charge his mobile devices as he traveled.

Mogadishu had been thrown into chaos by the collapse of the Somali Democratic Republic, torn by decades of civil war. Warlords eager to claim the foreign aid promised by developed nations struggled to establish themselves as the new central government to the exclusion of all others. But as the developed nations began to collapse themselves, the promise of foreign aid disappeared, and with it the incentive for civil war. New Mogadishu had been raised out of the ashes of the old city. Commerce returned, and with it, new prosperity. The lure of completely free trade drew both local entrepreneurs and foreign investors. New Mogadishu quickly became a bustling metropolis, and the telecommunications capital of the world.

Hakim worked as a programmer for Krito Communications. Krito had begun in the US, shielding customers from government attempts to acquire their phone records by every legal means available. They'd then developed numerous encryption algorithms to secure the privacy of their customers' data. But as populist revolutions began springing up around the world, they'd recognized the urgent need for telecommunications that could not be interrupted or intercepted by existing governments. Establishing their headquarters in New Mogadishu had made that possible, and Krito quickly became the world's largest, most impenetrable data haven.

In addition, Krito had launched a private currency called Kred that quickly became the international standard for Internet commerce. Recognizing the role of hyperinflation in the global economic collapse, Krito had designed the Kred to be entirely digital, which had numerous advantages. First, it could not be manipulated by inflation, because the supply was fixed based on the total number of transactions occurring in the system. Second, it could be transferred using any Krito Communications device, from mobile phones to vehicle GPS systems. The third, and perhaps most innovative advantage, was that Kred represented both "credit" and "credibility." Built into each transaction was an approval rating so that users all have a published reputation evaluation. If users lost their credibility due to dishonest business practices, their Kred was devalued accordingly. The result was an untraceable, decentralized, internationally accepted currency that governments could neither seize nor stop.

The Pirate Bigh

When Hakim arrived at work, he logged into a half dozen social networking sites. This was actually encouraged by his employer, the idea being that frequent mental micro-breaks leave employees more refreshed and creative than a rigid break schedule does. Internet access was his favorite perk, which he used to manage his more entrepreneurial online activities. This was also encouraged. Krito's policy was that allowing thousands of employees to test their ideas in the market directly was the most fluid laboratory for research and development. The Krito Communications office was a truly modern work environment. Their philosophy was that any free time an employee acquired by completing their regular responsibilities ahead of schedule belonged to them, and that this would not only encourage efficient time management, but everyone would mutually benefit from allowing innovation at all levels of the company.

A message popped onto Hakim's home screen. It was a request from his department head to come to her office. When he walked in, Rose asked him to close the door and have a seat. Whenever this happened, Hakim felt a lurch in the pit of his stomach. There was something about authority itself that made him uneasy. It usually passed as soon as Rose explained the purpose of the meeting.

"I want to talk to you about transferring to a new position in client relations. It would mean a 30,000,000-Kred raise, but there's potentially a whale of a client on the line. It would mean a lot more responsibility."

Rose seemed unusually humble, even conciliatory. Something had spooked her.

"I don't really know that much about client relations. I'm happy to try, but why are you offering this position to me?" Hakim asked.

"The client asked for you by name. But I don't want to say too much. It's better if he tells you himself." She gave him instructions to meet with the client, a man named Beigh, upstairs in the executive lounge.

Hakim ventured into the huge circular room, glancing admiringly at the view from the tall windows overlooking New Mogadishu. People from around the world, speaking dozens of languages, met here to eat and socialize between meetings. Some business travelers actually landed on the rough and never went below the executive lounge. A sense of privacy was still maintained by the sheer vastness of the space. Hakim was clearly out of place, both for his age and his clothes—there was no dress code in the programming office. Even the waitstaff looked more professional than he did.

Across the room a man stood waving to Hakim. Hakim noted that he was unusually tall, like the Mandinka people in West Africa, and dressed all in white, with a dark midnight-black complexion. He extended his hand, with its long round fingers, and shook Hakim's.

"You must be Hakim! I am Beigh. I am very excited to meet you. Please, sit down. Order whatever you like."

Beigh motioned to the menu as Hakim took a seat across from him and began to browse the selections. He'd never eaten anywhere so expensive, or with such diverse cuisine. He wondered if Beigh knew that the custom in New Mogadishu was for the person who extended the invitation to foot the bill. He thought it better not risk it, but even the appetizers were over 20,000 Kred.

Beigh asked, "Do you mind if I conduct a small test of... cognitive ability?" Hakim agreed. "Excellent! Just keep reading the menu. You won't feel a thing."

Beigh popped up and removed some kind of mobile device from his pocket. It looked like a smart phone, or maybe a camera. He held it up to Hakim's head as he walked around the table, and a detailed schematic of the inside of Hakim's brain appeared on the screen.

"Beautiful! Just as I'd hoped," Beigh exclaimed.

"What is it?"

"Your brain. It's marvelous. Not a bruise. Not a hint of scar tissue."

"Scar tissue?" Hakim jumped up, rubbing the back of his head with one hand. "How are you looking in my head?"

Beigh snapped the device closed. "Oh, Hakim. I have so much to share with you! But first I must ask you... do you want to live on a free world?"

"Of course..."

"Good. Let me show you something." Beigh set the device on the table and activated some kind of a projector that suspended a holographic screen above the table. Far more advanced than anything Krito was even close to. The display scrolled through scenes from science fiction movies. A flying saucer demolishing a building with an energy beam. Rows of green men marching in lockstep. A cartoon Martian training his crosshairs on Earth. Laser battles and bug armies, and on and on.

The movie clips scrolled on as Beigh continued. "Do you know what all these stories have in common, Hakim?"

"Aliens?"

"Well, yes. But more than that, they all represent tragic expressions of a primitive psychoclass. They contain depictions of xenophobia, species supremacy, and naked collectivism. On this planet, inter-terrestrial individuals are presumed to be hostile, hive-minded, and fundamentally defined by their planet of birth, rather than by the content of their character. Frankly it's obscene."

"What's your point? I don't understand what you're getting at."

Beigh laughed softly. "No. I suppose you wouldn't. The point is that I am prepared to deliver hundreds, maybe thousands of foreign merchants, bringing fantastic new technology to this market, but the aggregate of them are only going to feel comfortable trading here if I can demonstrate that a new psychoclass is being born here."

Hakim mulled it over and asked, "Thousands of foreign merchants coming... to Somalia?"

"No, Hakim... coming to Earth."

Hakim jumped back, wide-eyed. "You're an alien! What do

you want with me?"

"You are the key, Hakim. The brain scan shows it. I can spot the primitive psychoclass by physical changes in the brain. Scar tissue, really. Adverse childhood experiences cause decreased activity in the prefrontal cortex and a hyperactive amygdala. Tribalism, nationalism, bigotry—these are the symptoms of a damaged brain. A brain incapable of natural empathy. You've probably been told this behavior is normal because every generation of your species until now has shared these traits. But if you're brain scan is any indication something about this has always seemed flawed to you. You are different. I'm sure you've sensed it. You are the proof, maybe the first of your kind, that a generation is coming to this planet that is on the path to Astaiwah."

"Where is Astaiwah?"

"I forget... it has no equivalent in your language. Astaiwah is not a place. It is a direction. It is the future that is approached by the tendency of all sentient life that seeks harmony and autonomy. It is the aggregate of all consensual, mutually beneficial associations."

"What do I have to do?"

"Well... first, you need to see my world."

Alou Randon *Alou Randon is a writer and musician whose piece "The Capitalist Party" was inspired by the Marxist theory of commodity fetishism as well as the Trotskyist theory of state capitalism. Randon's website is alou-randon.com.*

THE CAPITALIST PARTY

by Alou Randon

Capitalist youth organize marching through the streets regurgitating the altruistic latest plastered on billboards all fed through the Bureaucratic Hippy for maximum relevance. America sings its anthem to the dollar grand protector of all that is good and free.

The Minutiæ Department monitor all the current political goings-on, charting the monetary value of each ideology trying to work out which one's going to be the new black.

"A price to everything and to everything its right price."

The Bureaucratic Hippy steps up to the pedestal, crowd of sycophants cheering. His attire changes automatically with the times, always encompassing the proper amalgamation of brands to ensure peak capital. He starts to speak :

"Do you tire of this world of subjectives and intangibles ?"

he cell phones in the audience beep and chime in agreement.

A member of the Minutiæ Department pitches a stand in the wings selling ideologies, marking up prices as their values change. Each and every one of them's primed and packaged so as to be palatable for the masses. "Anti-authoritarianism for sale! Conservatism 50% off — Everything must go !" New order of libertinism's arrived bearing the hallmarks of Rimbaud and Kerouac so everyone can carry the same sophistication.

"I will make it my goal to simplify the world, to reduce everything to absolutes and trend. How am I going to do this, you ask? I present to you the machine of now!"

A sleek piece of machinery, encrusted with switches and dials, whirs away beside him.

"It can convert everything to pure capital. A label, a person, an ideology — anything can be scanned in and be converted to pure monetary value."

A pack of cigarettes volunteers to be typified. He stands beside the machine as it pries him to bits. The audience laughs in their sleeves as he is revealed to be inauthentic. He has not seen this, he has not heard that.

The It Girl joins him on the stage. She waves and smiles as the audience chants God Save The It Girl, Bureaucratic Hippy saying "I present to you the representative of modern times !"

"This could be you," he says hype-mongering the masses, soon-to-become relics of capital in accordance with the now… presentation is everything, personality gleaned from every label displayed…

Mumurs of approval fill the crowd. A pair of glasses strikes up a conversation with a cup of coffee. "She's got a face that sells manifestos," Say the glasses.

The coffee cup scrutinizes the glasses. He nods in agreement while he blacklists them as inauthentic.

The crowd knows the It Girl's face from magazines, her image repurposed for every product imaginable. The It Girl uses it because it is hip, and it is hip because the It Girl uses it.

"Get with the times," she says, speaking in buzzwords and slogans, posing with coffee cups and pairs of shoes, pulling herself up by the most fashionably tailored pair of bootstraps.

The Minutiæ Department preach brevity for charity tacked onto every missive to drive up public image.

"Who really has time to analyze everything so thoroughly? Good person bad person, who can tell if not for the brands displayed? Thus we introduce the compressed existence."

The Bureaucratic Hippy lowers his tone. "This does of course raise some difficult questions. In a world where everything is measured in the same way, what is the value of a person ?" He scans himself into the machine and reads from the screen. "One thousand, five hundred fifty-three dollars and ninety-five cents."

He displays a relic of the past on the screen, yesterday's news conglomerated into a person, and sure enough the glasses in the audience retch, they recoil in horror at this irrelevant man.

The Bureaucratic Hippy scans in the common shoe. A crass display of artlessness fills the screen, audience averting their eyes.

"The machine is always right," Quips the It Girl.

The Bureaucratic Hippy scans in an old masterpiece and deems it irrelevant in this world of the now. He throws the painting to the audience. They fall upon it and rip it to shreds.

"Are we not predators ?" They say, "Instinct compels us to act as we do and who are you to intervene on instinct…"

The entrepreneurial primate lumbers across the screen. He beats his chest, he throws his shit, he invests capital to expand his business. "Naturalism at its finest."

The zeitgeist changes before the crowd's eyes as the Bureaucratic Hippy flicks switches self-consuming trend chasing itself around line graphs before crashing headfirst into passé.

"You are a rational actor," The Bureaucratic Hippy assures the audience. "And surely a rational actor such as yourself would allow no malfunction in the system."

Nonetheless they panic as they uniformly realize that they are not with the times. One of them sounds the alarm, discordant blips and chirps filling the arena as the crowd pull the Bureaucratic Hippy down from his pedestal and tear his clothes to shreds while the It Girl stands in place blowing kisses and waving.

"No need to panic this is a false alarm…"

They grasp at swatches of fabric trying to cover themselves so as to avoid fatal irrelevance.

The member of the Minutiæ Department vacates his stand and escorts the It Girl off the stage with her still repeating "No need to panic…"

Back at the department headquarters they flip a switch on the back of her neck and she stops dead in her tracks, head hanging low as they open her up and rewire her, changing her tastes and beliefs.

"She'll be a libertine this time around," one says. "It'll be good for product endorsements."

Another says "I still think she'd be better suited to anarchy" but the rest scoff.

"It's had its day in the sun."

CEO Darkhorse has made the town his. The windows are full of his neon signs, every citizen vying for his brand. They have absorbed into themselves his ideology. Other CEOs stop dead in their tracks with the crushing realization of irrelevance. Their posses follow suit, falling to their knees gasping. Darkhorse looks up with a smirk :

"There's a new sheriff in town."

75

Ric Driver grew up on Mars. His body was in Colorado at the time, but through Bradbury, Clarke, Asimov and others, he spent most evenings on Mars, Arrakis, Pern, and other pleasant educational places. Returning mostly to Earth in the seventies, he continued growing up in Santa Barbara, and is currently continuing the process of growing up, out, on, sideways, and inward in Iowa.

THE 3 LITTLE PIGS: PART 2

by Ric Driver

After the first winter in their new, solid brick house, the three little pigs sat in front of the big fireplace eating breakfast.

"Well, we survived the winter. The wolf didn't get us," said the first little pig.

"He didn't eat us, anyway. But look at all the firewood we had to buy from him to heat the house," said the third. "This house is strong and all, but it gets cold as soon as the fire dies down. How can we survive the next winter if the wolf raises his prices? I miss your straw house; it was so warm."

"Yes. We weren't shivering every morning. I just wish it hadn't been so flimsy." replied the first.

The second little pig mused, "My stick house was pretty good for that, but when the wind was blowing, those drafts went right down my back. It was cheap to build and it held the roof up really well, though."

As the sun began to come in through the southeast window, warming them a little, the light dawned.

"What if we built a new house, one with the best parts of the first three?"

They built an open frame of stout sticks, and put a solid roof on it. They harvested straw and tied it into large bundles, which they stacked like bricks from floor to ceiling between the sticks. They mortared the inside and outside of the walls to keep the straw in place and seal out the wind. They put large windows on the south side of the house to let in free heat from the sun.

The wolf watched all this with dismay, trying to think of a new way to get to the pigs. He finally gave up, and started an organic permaculture garden. To his surprise, he liked it very much, because it was so much easier to grow food himself than to do all that chasing and blowing.

Every summer after that, the pigs would look down the road

and run into the house, laughing and saying, "Here he comes again!" as the wolf huffed and puffed, pushing his heavy wheelbarrow toward their house.

"Little pigs, little pigs, I know you're home! Come on, won't you please take some of my extra zucchini?"

And they all coexisted sustainably ever after.

F.J. Bergmann frequents Wisconsin and fibitz.com. She is the editor of Star*Line, the journal of the Science Fiction Poetry Association (sfpoetry.com), and the poetry editor of Mobius: The Journal of Social Change (mobiusmagazine.com). Her most recent chapbook, an illustrated collection of conflated-fairy-tale poems, is Out of the Black Forest (Centennial Press, 2012).

MEASURING UP

by F.J. Bergmann

1. Rules are for other people.
2. Rulers are for other people, on other continents.
3. Rulers shall use only pixels as units and shall be inscribed on only one side. In order to not waste sides, all rulers shall be manufactured as Möbius strips. The penalty for bisecting a ruler laterally shall be confounded by early withdrawal. The penalty for bisecting a ruler longitudinally shall be confusion.
4. There are special rules for sex.
5. There are special rulers for sex characteristics.
6. There are special rules for continents and incontinents.
7. The rules you favor are in disfavor.
8. The rulers you favor have fallen out of fashion. So have their units. See Rule 3, up there somewhere.
9. Rules don't kill people; rulers kill people.
10. The Golden Rule turned out to have a superficial gilt coating which scraped off easily.

RicardoFeral is an analog dinosaur in the digital jungle. Writer, anarcho-agrarian, repairman and builder of neat stuff. Bringing 3rd world technology to the 1st world. feral-tech.com

SILENT NIGHT
by Ricardo Feral

I have to admit, I was sick of the drones. Police drones, sanitation enforcement quad-rotors, and now even the advert-drones–collecting data on every aspect of life. Buzzing, humming, always present, always watching. Even in our cul-de-sac at the far edge of town, the never-ending noise of the drones was getting... just plain annoying.

My neighbor, well, I guess he had just had enough.

We residents of Turkey Creek Hollow are primarily Anarcaps, with a smattering of other anarcho-hyphens of one flavor or another. Anarcho-capitalists, anarcho-syndicalists, anarcho-feminists etcetera etcetera. Mostly home-schooled or un-schooled, young, gifted and semi-white, grandkids of what was once the middle class. The Anarcaps seem especially drawn to the cheap, split level duplexes–by genetics, I think. None of us are old enough to have experienced the internally-combusted lifestyle that took place in these winding subdivisions and cul de sacs, and yet we feel somehow drawn to the mandelbrot arrangements of "Lanes", "Drives", "Vistas", "Views", "Trails" and "Runs" that metastasized across what was once farmland, virgin prairie and oak savannah–before everything went–quite literally–south. Unlike the anarchosyndics, who gravitate to the collective living in old industrial buildings or downtown row houses and the shared labor of inner-city farming, we anarcaps like to have our space. Our own little space. I guess it's just in our nature.

Turkey Creek Hollow is a cul-de-sac off of Elmview, just north of the Herbert Hoover Expressway and south of Holiday Trail. The street is lined with split-level duplexes of similar design, descending the hillside toward the expressway and then winding its way back to reconnect to itself, forming a noose-shaped ribbon of decaying concrete. The houses are in varying states of disrepair ranging from minor hail-damaged vinyl siding to burned-out shells, and the yards are overgrown with silver maples, staghorn sumac, stinging nettle and burdock. A few of the houses are obviously occupied and those yards boast rambling vegetable gardens, fruit and nut trees, or berry bushes. If it weren't for the drones, it would have been quite idyllic. But hey, those fucking things are everywhere, these days.

We claimed squatters rights on a split level duplex at the bottom of the hill last spring. It was a legal occupation under the T.R.Z. (Tax Reclamation Zone) law, but frankly, there is no enforcement to throw us out, even if it wasn't legal. No one cared about about Turkey Creek Hollow, it seemed, and that is just what we were looking for.

At this point, I should explain that when I say "We", I mean MannyMo and Jaques, Girly-Girl and me. I'm Hairy. I mean, they call me Hairy. The four of us met in an agorist squat downtown, but none of us really fit in to the whole polyamorous scene down there. Not that any of us are so squidgy or uptight–it's just that the Pep Boys (MannyMo and Jaques) were a pretty committed pair, and Girly-Girl, I don't really know what she's into. I'm thinking there is some deep, dark shit going on there. And me, well...none of that is important to this story. Suffice it to say that the vegan food was great and the squat was warm and friendly, but the four of us weren't into sharing a case of genital warts with a whole lotta dumpster-divin' freegans–no offense. We just never really fit in, and we tended to hang together, the four of us.

Girly-Girl knew some anarcaps and privateers who had found their way out to the farthest reaches of suburbia, and word had it that living was good. If you don't mind the drones.

When we took possession of the squat on Turkey Creek Hollow, we noticed Burl immediately. He was hard to miss.

First, there weren't many older people in this particular T.R.Z. Burl stood out among the smooth-faced suburban pioneers, with his bushy white beard, pale blue eyes set deep in brown, deeply creased face shaded by a dingy meshback cap with the word "Mötorhead" printed on the front. His hair hung in a long yellowish-gray braid down his back to his tooled leather belt and, most notably, he had giant tufts of grey hair growing out of his ears. This grooming faux pas was amusingly disconcerting to even some of the younger, hairy arm-pitted and dreadlocked earth-mothers and trans-groovers on the block. It seemed that their acceptance of unconventional style choices did not extend to the old and un-ironic.

Then there was his car. An ancient, rusting hulk of a late 20th century Oldsmobile "Ninety-Eight," powered by a wood-gasifier. In an area mostly free of internal combustion engines, the beastly contraption cruised the cracked and crumbled streets of the sub-development with an enormous stainless steel kettle mounted on a steel diamond plate platform where the trunk used to be. It belched white smoke and as he drove past, the exhaust filled the neighborhood with the smell of a campfire. And always, the car was accompanied by a squadron of drones, sniffing the exhaust and photographing the long out-of-date license plates. I'm sure they also didn't miss his bumper stickers, including "Drones go Home" and "Personal Airspace Protected by Smith and Wesson."

Burl lives in the old farmhouse at the end of Holiday Trail. The original inhabitants of the farmstead had owned the fields and pastures that were now veined with suburban neighborhoods. From the road you could barely see the house, a rambling victorian with a second floor porch and dormers sprouting in every direction. The yard was mostly overgrown with trees, but above the trees you could see the rusting steel roof of a massive barn and two ancient windmills. One, with the word "Aeromotor" on the tail must have been used for water pumping, and the other a "Zenith" probably charged Burl's batteries. Burl had somehow managed to keep this tiny time capsule of early 20th century rural America intact long enough for the economic downturn to kill any further advancement.

At times, when Girly-Girl, the Pep Boys and I would walk the dogs along Holiday Trail, we would walk past Burl's gate, and try to be inconspicuous as we craned our necks in hopes of getting a glimpse of the inside of the compound. He always seemed to be working on something in there, but you couldn't really see through the overgrowth. The sounds of grinding metal, or the blue glow and crackle of a cutting torch would filter out to the street. The drones were always there, too, monitoring his activity from a safe distance.

"Be careful, the old fuck might shoot us!" Jaques would say– or something to that effect–as he would hurry past.

Girly-Girl was the most curious. "Look Jakey, the sign on the gate says clearly 'Government Agents Keep Out.' We aren't government agents! I think the old guy is sweet- he's just shy!"

I started to think Girly-Girl was right. Burl kept pretty much to himself, but occasionally MannyMo and I would see him down at the repair co-op and he alway gave us a tight-lipped smile and a nod, then head out back to the junk pile where he would quietly scrounge for engine parts, pieces of steel pipe or archaic electronic components. Still, I had never really talked to Burl, and our interactions had been limited friendly nods or a wave as he passed in the 98, so I was surprised when, late in November, Burl came to the door of our squat.

I woke to the sound of someone knocking at the door, rapping "shave and a haircut" on the fiberglass door with hard knuckles. The stocky little man with the Mötorhead hat was on our front stoop, smiling like the cat who just ate a canary.

"Hullo there." His voice was raspy and he had the rural accent of someone who hadn't watched enough television as a child. "I was wonderin'…" his voice was drowned out temporarily by the whining of a quad-rotor buzzing over the rooftop. He paused, and his friendly demeanor turned to a scowl as he looked angrily at the sky. As the sound faded, the smile returned and he continued. "I was wonderin'– did the folks that used to live here happen to leave behind any-ah them decorations they use-tah put up in the yard? You know, them blow-up jobees?"

MannyMo wandered to the door, rubbing the sleep from his eyes, and peeked over my shoulder at Burl. "What do you want with all of that old christmas junk, Burl? I mean, sir? Can we call you Burl?"

"I was plannin' ta do a little decoratin' this year- ya know, around the neighborhood'n'all. Figgered a fella could do a purty nice display with summa that old stuff."

I said that yes, among the stuff the former inhabitants had left behind were a pile of red and green plastic bins that contained what looked to be some inflatable snowmen ant the little blower motors to inflate them. Because we used a small solar array for our power, we had no use for the energy-sucking decorations–and besides, who wants a fucking inflatable snowman in their yard?

I opened the garage door. By this time the whole household was up, and excited to find that we had made contact with our wacky old neighbor. We all pitched in and helped him load the dusty bins onto a trailer (made from the back half of a Dodge pickup) that was hitched behind the smoking behemoth sedan. With electricity in short supply, I couldn't imagine that he was going to string Christ-mas lights across the neighborhood. But as his land barge disap-peared around the cul du sac in a cloud of smoke and a swarm of buzzing drones, I admit, my curiosity was piqued.

On the 24th of December, Girly-Girl and I took the dogs out just before sunset. There was the usual buzzing of drones, going about their endless daily duties- probing for open wireless networks, recording license plates, sniffing trashcans, recording where my dogs shit, sniffing said shit to determine if my dogs were up to date on their vaccinations, and then recording me picking up and dispos-ing of the shit in a legal manner. Goddamit, I thought, even out here in no-mans land, they were just looking for any excuse to send you to Prison Industries for a month.

We hadn't seen much of our new found friend Burl since his visit to the squat to collect the old Christmas decorations. We all had wondered in passing if he was actually going to pull off his plan to decorate the neighborhood, but so far, the signs of holiday cheer in the neighborhood were limited to red and green advert drones projecting holiday shopping specials onto the safety barricades at the bottom of the hill by the expressway. I had seen him once at the scrap heap and asked him how his plans were coming. "Purty Good." was all he offered in response, with that silly grin.

As Girly-Girl and the dogs reached the top of Turkey Creek Hollow and turned on to Holiday Trail, I saw the smoke in the dis-tance and heard the sound of Burl's car. The dogs began to bark wildly and their ears went back. Girly-Girl stopped in mid-stride, frozen in amazement.

"Oh Holy Shit!" she sputtered, and then began to laugh.

The 98 was towing a tethered flotilla of multicolored di-rigibles. Giant inflatable snowmen, Santa Clauses, candy canes, christmas trees, toy soldiers, reindeer, a couple of Grinches and a giant, inflatable baby Jesus trailed behind the car. As he approached he rolled down his window, gave a little two-fingered salute and grinned a giant grin.

"What ARE you doing?" I called out, as the dogs growled and barked at the flying lawn ornaments as they bobbed and strained at their cables, bumping into each other like an airborne mosh pit.

"Ever heard the song "Silent Night?" He said, as he rolled on.

He set about his task at an amazing speed. He dropped the weights made of five gallon plastic buckets full of dirt along Holiday Trail and releasing the inflatables so that they hovered about 60 feet in the air. They were interwoven with thin cables, and the sky over the neighborhood quickly began to fill with the cartoon characters, symbols of the bygone era of cheap petroleum products and religious self-expression through consumerism.

The crowd of curious residents was beginning to form in the street. The dreadlocked earth-mothers and the trans-groovers, the anarcaps and the agorists, the bikers and the hackers and the black-blocers from the end of the road, they all came out to watch with amazement and glee as the old man set about his task.

A traffic drone that was hovering overhead to observe the curious scene was the first to fall prey to the old man's plan. The monofilament tether of a giant plastic Grinch snagged the prop of the drone and sent it spinning to the ground and it skipped along the median, coming to rest against the curb. A parking enforcement quad-rotor narrowly missed colliding with an enormous flying wooden soldier, swerving and dipping, loosing control and crashing into a stop sign with a resounding "BONG!" There were gasps from the crowd, followed by nervous giggles, then chuckles, and finally... applause!

As darkness fell, the dirigibles sprung up block by block, until the entire neighborhood resembled a cross between the Macy's parade and the city of London during the blitz. By now, everyone in the area had come out to see it, riding there bikes and pulling their kids in wagons or on sleds. Friends gathered on their porches and gazed up at the holiday themed aerial defense network. As the drones fell, sparking and smoking, observers across the neighborhood began to give out collective "ooohs!" and "ahs!" and applauding, as if it were and Independence Day fireworks show. A few times the drones came down hard, right toward the crowd and they scattered and ran for cover under trees and behind fences. A few of the bikers and black-blocers began to run up the street, faces hidden from the cameras by black kerchiefs, hoodies and balaclavas, swatting at the disoriented drones with baseball bats and tennis rackets.

"Steee-rike two!" called a gleeful biker to his teammates.

It wasn't long before the humming grew quieter, as the drones adjusted to the obstacles, retreating to positions high above and outside the perimeter of our cheerful, vigilant, inflatable defenders and their deadly network of anti-aircraft cables. Soon, someone down the block began to sing. "Silent Night".

"Silent night, Holy night
All is calm, all is bright
Round yon virgin, mother and child
Holy infant so, tender and mild
Sleep in heavenly peace,
Sleep in heavenly peace.
Silent night, Holy night...."

A few others joined in, but it was half-hearted, and only a few could remember the words.

A calm fell over the neighborhood, and everything went silent. The bikers and black-blocers had worn themselves out and gone in search of beer. The earth-mothers took their tired children to bed. Soon, everyone wast back indoors, except for me, the Pep Boys and Girly-Girl.

I smelled woodsmoke, and heard the rumble of the Olds as it crept back toward the old farmhouse.

"The old man with the white beard was finished with his Christmas rounds." said Jaques.

"He sure as fuck ain't no Santy Clause," said Girly-Girl.

"You can't fool me, there ain't no Sanity Clause!" said MannyMo, and he went inside.

Girly-Girl and I sat on the stoop for a while, watching the stars come out. I imagined for a minute that Orion was battling the shadowy inflatable baby Jesus. After a while, I went inside and made a cup of tea, in the quiet of a drone-free Christmas eve. I fell asleep soundly, dreaming of Christmases long ago.

It was Christmas morning at sunrise when I took the dogs out again, and saw the Prison Industries work crews bringing down the holiday air raid blimps. The workers in their gray jumpsuits and electronic shock collars laughed and shook their heads as they packed the deflated Jesus into the back of a yellow pickup. Others swept up the shattered plastic bits of drones and quad-rotors and shoveled them into recycling cans. A few small, low flying drones were already back to work, hovering above my dogs to read their chips and catalog their bowel movements. The advert-drones down by the expressway blared distorted, echiong christmas music, compliments of their corporate sponsors.

SI-Si-silent NI-Ni-ight-ight,
HO-Ho-holy NI-Ni-night-ight,
FI-Fi-fifty Percent-ent-ent off-off-off,
VA-va-cation-on Flight-igh-ights....

As I reached the intersection of Turkey Creek Hollow and Holiday Trail, a line of police cruisers was pulling out of the driveway at the old house at the end of the street. I rushed over to the curb, and my heart sank.

In the backseat of the second car, I could see Burl. As they crept past, He turned his head to look at me. He smiled, raised his cuffed hands, flashed a peace sign and nodded the friendly nod. I smiled and waived back, and held my fist up in a lame-ass attempt at showing solidarity.

"You can't fool me, there ain't no Sanity Clause," I said, to no one in particular.

BLAIR GAUNTT

Philip Kindred Dick (1928–1982) PKD is one of the most influential science fiction writers in the history of the genre. His paradigm-busting visions of society and consciousness inspired an entire generation of writers and filmmakers. The Last of the Masters, aka Protection Agency, first appeared in Orbit Science Fiction in 1954.

THE LAST OF THE MASTERS
by Philip K. Dick

Consciousness collected around him. He returned with reluctance; the weight of centuries, an unbearable fatigue, lay over him. The ascent was painful. He would have shrieked if there were anything to shriek with. And anyhow, he was beginning to feel glad.

Eight thousand times he had crept back thus, with ever-increasing difficulty. Someday he wouldn't make it. Someday the black pool would remain. But not this day. He was still alive; above the aching pain and reluctance came joyful triumph.

"Good morning," a bright voice said. "Isn't it a nice day? I'll pull the curtains and you can look out."

He could see and hear. But he couldn't move. He lay quietly and allowed the various sensations of the room to pour in on him. Carpets, wallpaper, tables, lamps, pictures. Desk and vidscreen. Gleaming yellow sunlight streamed through the window. Blue sky. Distant hills. Fields, buildings, roads, factories. Workers and machines.

Peter Green was busily straightening things, his young face wreathed with smiles. "Lots to do today. Lots of people to see you. Bills to sign. Decisions to make. This is Saturday. There will be people coming in from the remote sectors. I hope the maintenance crew has done a good job." He added quickly, "They have, of course. I talked to Fowler on my way over here. Everything's fixed up fine."

The youth's pleasant tenor mixed with the bright sunlight. Sounds and sights, but nothing else. He could feel nothing. He tried to move his arm but nothing happened.

"Don't worry," Green said, catching his terror. "They'll soon be along with the rest. You'll be all right. You have to be. How could we survive without you?"

He relaxed. God knew, it had happened often enough before. Anger surged dully. Why couldn't they coordinate? Get it up all at once, not piece-meal. He'd have to change their schedule. Make them organize better.

Past the bright window a squat metal car chugged to a halt. Uniformed men piled out, gathered up heavy armloads of equipment, and hurried toward the main entrance of the building.

"Here they come," Green exclaimed with relief. "A little late, eh?"

"Another traffic tie-up," Fowler snorted, as he entered. "Something wrong with the signal system again. Outside flow got mixed up with the urban stuff; tied up on all sides. I wish you'd change the law."

Now there was motion all around him. The shapes of Fowler and McLean loomed, two giant moons abruptly ascendant. Professional faces that peered down at him anxiously. He was turned over on his side. Muffled conferences. Urgent whispers. The clank of tools.

"Here," Fowler muttered. "Now here. No, that's later. Be careful. Now run it up through here."

The work continued in taut silence. He was aware of their closeness. Dim outlines occasionally cut off his light. He was turned this way and that, thrown around like a sack of meal.

"Okay," Fowler said. "Tape it."

A long silence. He gazed dully at the wall, at the slightly-faded blue and pink wallpaper. An old design that showed a woman in hoop skirts, with a little parasol over her dainty shoulder. A frilly white blouse, tiny tips of shoes. An astoundingly clean puppy at her side.

Then he was turned back, to face upward. Five shapes groaned and strained over him. Their fingers flew, their muscles rippled under their shirts. At last they straightened up and retreated. Fowler wiped sweat from his face; they were all tense and bleary eyed.

"Go ahead," Fowler rasped. "Throw it."

Shock hit him. He gasped. His body arched, then settled slowly down.

His body. He could feel. He moved his arms experimentally. He touched his face, his shoulder, the wall. The wall was real and hard. All at once the world had become three-dimensional again.

Relief showed on Fowler's face. "Thank God." He sagged wearily. "How do you feel?"

After a moment he answered, "All right."

Fowler sent the rest of the crew out. Green began dusting again, off in the corner. Fowler sat down on the edge of the bed and lit his pipe. "Now listen to me," he said. "I've got bad news. I'll give it to you the way you always want it, straight from the shoulder."

"What is it?" he demanded. He examined his fingers. He already knew.

There were dark circles under Fowler's eyes. He hadn't shaved. His square-jawed face was drawn and unhealthy. "We were up all night. Working on your motor system. We've got it jury-rigged,

but it won't hold. Not more than another few months. The thing's climbing. The basic units can't be replaced. When they wear out they're gone. We can weld in relays and wiring, but we can't fix the five synapsis-coils. There were only a few men who could make those, and they've been dead two centuries. If the coils burn out --"

"Is there any deterioration in the synapsis-coils?" he interrupted.

"Not yet. Just motor areas. Arms, in particular. What's happening to your legs will happen to your arms and finally all your motor system. You'll be paralyzed by the end of the year. You'll be able to see, hear, and think. And broadcast. But that's all." He added, "Sorry, Bors. We're doing all we can."

"All right," Bors said. "You're excused. Thanks for telling me straight. I guessed."

"Ready to go down? A lot of people with problems, today. They're stuck until you get there."

"Let's go." He focused his mind with an effort and turned his attention to the details of the day. "I want the heavy metals research program speeded. It's lagging, as usual. I may have to pull a number of men from related work and shift them to the generators. The water level will be dropping soon. I want to start feeding power along the lines while there's still power to feed. As soon as I turn my back everything starts falling apart."

Fowler signaled Green and he came quickly over. The two of them bent over Bors and, grunting, hoisted him up and carried him to the door. Down the corridor and outside.

They deposited him in the squat metal car, the new little service truck. Its polished surface was a startling contrast to his pitted, corroded hull, bent and splotched and eaten away. A dull, patina-covered machine of archaic steel and plastic that hummed faintly, rustily, as the men leaped in the front seat and raced the car out onto the main highway.

Edward Tolby perspired, pushed his pack up higher, hunched over, tightened his gun belt, and cursed.

"Daddy," Silvia reproved. "Cut that."

Tolby spat furiously in the grass at the side of the road. He put his arm around his slim daughter. "Sorry, Silv. Nothing personal. The damn heat."

Mid-morning sun shimmered down on the dusty road. Clouds of dust rose and billowed around the three as they pushed slowly along. They were dead tired. Tolby's heavy face was flushed and sullen. An unlit cigarette dangled between his lips. His big, power- fully built body was hunched resentfully forward. His daughter's canvas shirt clung moistly to her arms and breasts. Moons of sweat darkened her back. Under her jeans her thigh muscles rippled wea- rily.

Robert Penn walked a little behind the two Tolby's, hands deep in his pockets, eyes on the road ahead. His mind was blank; he was half asleep from the double shot of hexobarb he had swallowed at the last League camp. And the heat lulled him. On each side of the road fields stretched out, pastures of grass and weeds, a few trees here and there. A tumbled-down farmhouse. The ancient rusting re- mains of a bomb shelter, two centuries old. Once, some dirty sheep.

"Sheep," Penn said. "They eat the grass too far down. It won't grow back."

"Now he's a farmer," Tolby said to his daughter.

"Daddy," Silvia snapped. "Stop being nasty."

"It's this heat. This damn heat." Tolby cursed again, loudly and futilely. "It's not worth it. For ten pinks I'd go back and tell them it was a lot of pig swill."

"Maybe it is, at that," Penn said mildly.

"All right, you go back," Tolby grunted. "You go back and tell them it's a lot of pig swill. They'll pin a medal on you. Maybe raise you up a grade."

Penn laughed. "Both of you shut up. There's some kind of town ahead."

Tolby's massive body straightened eagerly. "Where?" He shielded his eyes. "By God, he's right. A village. And it isn't a mirage. You see it, don't you?" His good humor returned and he rubbed his big hands together. "What say, Penn. A couple of beers, a few games of throw with some of the local peasants—maybe we can stay overnight." He licked his thick lips with anticipation. "Some of those village wenches, the kind that hang around the grog shops --"

"I know the kind you mean," Penn broke in. "The kind that are tired of doing nothing. Want to see the big commercial centers. Want to meet some guy that'll buy them mecho-stuff and take them places."

At the side of the road a farmer was watching them curiously. He had halted his horse and stood leaning on his crude plow, hat pushed back on his head.

"What's the name of this town?" Tolby yelled.

The farmer was silent a moment. He was an old man, thin and weathered. "This town?" he repeated.

"Yeah, the one ahead."

"That's a nice town." The farmer eyed the three of them. "You been through here before?"

"No, sir," Tolby said. "Never."

"Team break down?"

"No, we're on foot."

"How far you come?"

"About a hundred and fifty miles."

The farmer considered the heavy packs strapped on their backs. Their cleated hiking shoes. Dusty clothing and weary, sweat-streaked faces. Jeans and canvas shirts. Ironite walking staffs. "That's a long way," he said. "How far you going?"

"As far as we feel like it," Tolby answered. "Is there a place ahead we can stay? Hotel? Inn?"

"That town," the farmer said, "is Fairfax. It has a lumber mill, one of the best in the world. A couple of pottery works. A place where you can get clothes put together by machines. Regular mecho-clothing. A gun shop where they pour the best shot this side of the Rockies. And a bakery. Also there's an old doctor living there, and a lawyer. And some people with books to teach the kids. They came with t.b. They made a school house out of an old barn."

"How large a town?" Penn asked.

"Lot of people. More born all the time. Old folks die. Kids die. We had a fever last year. About a hundred kids died. Doctor said it came from the water hole. We shut the water hole down. Kids died anyhow. Doctor said it was the milk. Drove off half the cows. Not mine. I stood out there with my gun and I shot the first of them came to drive off my cow. Kids stopped dying as soon as fall came. I think it was the heat."

"Sure is hot," Tolby agreed.

"Yes, it gets hot around here. Water's pretty scarce." A crafty look slid across his old face. "You folks want a drink? The young lady looks pretty tired. Got some bottles of water down under the house. In the mud. Nice and cold." He hesitated. "Pink a glass."

Tolby laughed. "No, thanks."

"Two glasses a pink," the farmer said.

"Not interested," Penn said. He thumped his canteen and the three of them started on. "So long."

The farmer's face hardened. "Damn foreigners," he muttered. He turned angrily back to his plowing.

The town baked in silence. Flies buzzed and settled on the backs of stupefied horses, tied up at posts. A few cars were parked here and there. People moved listlessly along the sidewalks. Elderly lean-bodied men dozed on porches. Dogs and chickens slept in the shade under houses. The houses were small, wooden, chipped and peeling boards, leaning and angular—and old. Warped and split by age and heat. Dust lay over everything. A thick blanket of dry dust over the cracking houses and the dull-faced men and animals.

Two lank men approached them from an open doorway. "Who are you? What do you want?"

They stopped and got out their identification. The men examined the sealed-plastic cards. Photographs, fingerprints, data. Finally they handed them back.

"AL," one said. "You really from the Anarchist League?"

"That's right," Tolby said.

"Even the girl?" The men eyed Silvia with languid greed. "Tell you what. Let us have the girl a while and we'll skip the head tax."

"Don't kid me," Tolby grunted. "Since when does the League pay head tax or any other tax?" He pushed past them impatiently. "Where's the grog shop? I'm dying!"

A two-story white building was on their left. Men lounged on the porch, watching them vacantly. Penn headed toward it and the Tolby's followed. A faded, peeling sign lettered across the front read: Beer, Wine on Tap.

"This is it," Penn said. He guided Silvia up the sagging steps, past the men, and inside. Tolby followed; he unstrapped his pack gratefully as he came.

The place was cool and dark. A few men and women were at the bar; the rest sat around tables. Some youths were playing throw in the back. A mechanical tune-maker wheezed and composed in the corner, a shabby, half-ruined machine only partially functioning. Behind the bar a primitive scene-shifter created and destroyed vague phantasmagoria: seascapes, mountain peaks, snowy valleys, great rolling hills, a nude woman that lingered and then dissolved into one vast breast. Dim, uncertain processions that no one noticed or looked at. The bar itself was an incredibly ancient sheet of transparent plastic, stained and chipped and yellow with age. Its n-grav coat had faded from one end; bricks now propped it up. The drink mixer had long since fallen apart. Only wine and beer were served. No living man knew how to mix the simplest drink.

Tolby moved up to the bar. "Beer," he said. "Three beers." Penn and Silvia sank down at a table and removed their packs, as the bartender served Tolby three mugs of thick, dark beer. He showed his card and carried the mugs over to the table.

The youths in the back had stopped playing. They were watching the three as they sipped their beer and unlaced their hiking boots. After a while one of them came slowly over.

"Say," he said. "You're from the League."

"That's right," Tolby murmured sleepily.

Everyone in the place was watching and listening. The youth sat down across from the three; his companions flocked excitedly around and took seats on all sides. The juveniles of the town. Bored, restless, dissatisfied. Their eyes took in the ironite staffs, the guns, the heavy metal-cleated boots. A murmured whisper rustled through them. They were about eighteen. Tanned, rangy.

"How do you get in?" one demanded bluntly.

"The League?" Tolby leaned back in his chair, found a match, and lit his cigarette. He unfastened his belt, belched loudly, and settled back contentedly. "You get in by examination."

"What do you have to know?"

Tolby shrugged. "About everything." He belched again and scratched thoughtfully at his chest, between two buttons. He was conscious of the ring of people around on all sides. A little old man with a beard and horn-rimmed glasses. At another table, a great tub of a man in a red shirt and blue-striped trousers, with a bulging stomach.

Youths. Farmers. A Negro in a dirty white shirt and trousers, a book under his arm. A hard-jawed blonde, hair in a net, red nails and high heels, tight yellow dress. Sitting with a gray-haired businessman in a dark brown suit. A tall young man holding hands with a young black-haired girl, huge eyes, in a soft white blouse and skirt, little slippers kicked under the table. Under the table her bare, tanned feet twisted; her slim body was bent forward with interest.

"You have to know," Tolby said, "how the League was formed. You have to know how we pulled down the governments that day. Pulled them down and destroyed them. Burned all the buildings. And all the records. Billions of microfilms and papers. Great bonfires that burned for weeks. And the swarms of little white things that poured out when we knocked the buildings over."

"You killed them?" the great tub of a man asked, lips twitching avidly.

"We let them go. They were harmless. They ran and hid. Under rocks." Tolby laughed. "Funny little scurrying things. Insects. Then we went in and gathered up all the records and equipment for making records. By God, we burned everything."

"And the robots," a youth said.

"Yeah, we smashed all the government robots. There weren't many of them. They were used only at high levels. When a lot of facts had to be integrated."

The youth's eyes bulged. "You saw them? You were there when they smashed the robots?" Penn laughed. "Tolby means the League. That was two hundred years ago."

The youth grinned nervously. "Yeah. Tell us about the marches."

Tolby drained his mug and pushed it away. "I'm out of beer."

The mug was quickly refilled. He grunted his thanks and continued, voice deep and furry, dulled with fatigue. "The marches. That was really some-thing, they say. All over the world, people getting up, throwing down what they were doing --"

"It started in East Germany," the hard-jawed blonde said. "The riots."

"Then it spread to Poland," the Negro put in shyly. "My grandfather used to tell me how everybody sat and listened to the television. His grandfather used to tell him. It spread to Czechoslovakia and then Austria and Romania and Bulgaria. Then France. And Italy."

"France was first!" the little old man with beard and glasses cried violently. "They were without a government a whole month. The people saw they could live without a government!"

"The marches started it," the black-haired girl corrected. "That was the first time they started pulling down the government buildings. In East Ger-many and Poland. Big mobs of unorganized workers."

"Russia and America were the last," Tolby said. "When the march on Washington came there was close to twenty million of us. We were big in those days! They couldn't stop us when we finally moved."

"They shot a lot," the hard-faced blonde said.

"Sure. But the people kept coming. And yelling to the soldiers. 'Hey, Bill! Don't shoot!' 'Hey, Jack! It's me, Joe.' 'Don't shoot— we're your friends!' 'Don't kill us, join us!' And by God, after a while they did. They couldn't keep shooting their own people. They finally threw down their guns and got out of the way."

"And then you found the place," the little black-haired girl said breathlessly.

"Yeah. We found the place. Six places. Three in America. One in Britain. Two in Russia. It took us ten years to find the last place--- and make sure it was the last place."

"What then?" the youth asked, bug-eyed.

"Then we busted every one of them." Tolby raised himself up, a massive man, beer mug clutched, heavy face flushed dark red. "Every damn A-bomb in the whole world."

There was an uneasy silence.

"Yeah," the youth murmured. "You sure took care of those war people."

"Won't be any more of them," the great tub of a man said. "They're gone for good."

Tolby fingered his ironite staff. "Maybe so. And maybe not. There just might be a few of them left."

"What do you mean?" the tub of a man demanded.

Tolby raised his hard gray eyes. "It's time you people stopped kidding us. You know damn well what I mean. We've heard rumors. Someplace around this area there's a bunch of them. Hiding out."

Shocked disbelief, then anger hummed to a roar. "That's a lie!" the tub of a man shouted.

"Is it?"

The little man with beard and glasses leaped up. "There's nobody here has anything to do with governments! We're all good people!"

"You better watch your step," one of the youths said softly to Tolby. "People around here don't like to be accused."

Tolby got unsteadily to his feet, his ironite staff gripped. Penn got up beside him and they stood together. "If any of you knows something," Tolby said, "you better tell it. Right now."

"Nobody knows anything," the hard-faced blonde said. "You're talking to honest folks."

"That's so," the Negro said, nodding his head. "Nobody here's doing anything wrong."

"You saved our lives," the black-haired girl said. "If you hadn't pulled down the governments we'd all be dead in the war. Why should we hold back something?"

"That's true," the great tub of a man grumbled. "We wouldn't be alive if it wasn't for the League. You think we'd do anything against the League?"

"Come on," Silvia said to her father. "Let's go." She got to her feet and tossed Penn his pack.

Tolby grunted belligerently. Finally he took his own pack and hoisted it to his shoulder. The room was deathly silent. Everyone stood frozen, as the three gathered their things and moved toward the door.

The little dark-haired girl stopped them. "The next town is thirty miles from here," she said.

"The road's blocked," her tall companion explained. "Slides

closed it years ago."

"Why don't you stay with us tonight? There's plenty of room at our place. You can rest up and get an early start tomorrow."

"We don't want to impose," Silvia murmured.

Tolby and Penn glanced at each other, then at the girl. "If you're sure you have plenty of room --"

The great tub of a man approached them. "Listen. I have ten yellow slips. I want to give them to the League. I sold my farm last year. I don't need any more slips; I'm living with my brother and his family." He pushed the slips at Tolby. "Here."

Tolby pushed them back. "Keep them."

"This way," the tall young man said, as they clattered down the sagging steps, into a sudden blinding curtain of heat and dust. "We have a car. Over this way. An old gasoline car. My dad fixed it so it burns oil."

"You should have taken the slips," Penn said to Tolby, as they got into the ancient, battered car. Flies buzzed around them. They could hardly breathe; the car was a furnace. Silvia fanned herself with a rolled-up paper. The black-haired girl unbuttoned her blouse.

"What do we need money for?" Tolby laughed good-natured-ly. "I haven't paid for anything in my life. Neither have you."

The car sputtered and moved slowly forward, onto the road. It began to gain speed. Its motor banged and roared. Soon it was moving surprisingly fast.

"You saw them," Silvia said, over the racket. "They'd give us anything they had. We saved their lives." She waved at the fields, the farmers and their crude teams, the withered crops, the sagging old farmhouses. "They'd all be dead, if it hadn't been for the League." She smashed a fly peevishly. "They depend on us."

The black-haired girl turned toward them, as the car rushed along the decaying road. Sweat streaked her tanned skin. Her half-covered breasts trembled with the motion of the car. "I'm Laura Davis. Pete and I have an old farmhouse his dad gave us when we got married."

"You can have the whole downstairs," Pete said.

"There's no electricity, but we've got a big fireplace. It gets cold at night. It's hot in the day, but when the sun sets it gets terribly cold."

"We'll be all right," Penn murmured. The vibration of the car made him a little sick.

"Yes," the girl said, her black eyes flashing. Her crimson lips twisted. She leaned toward Penn intently, her small face strangely alight. "Yes, we'll take good care of you."

At that moment the car left the road.

Silvia shrieked. Tolby threw himself down, head between his knees, doubled up in a ball. A sudden curtain of green burst around Penn. Then a sickening emptiness, as the car plunged down. It struck with a roaring crash that blotted out everything. A single titanic cataclysm of fury that picked Penn up and flung his remains in every direction.

"Put me down," Bors ordered. "On this railing for a moment before I go inside."

The crew lowered him onto the concrete surface and fastened magnetic grapples into place. Men and women hurried up the wide steps, in and out of the massive building that was Bors' main offices.

The sight from these steps pleased him. He liked to stop here and look around at his world. At the civilization he had carefully constructed. Each piece added painstakingly, scrupulously with infinite care, throughout the years.

It wasn't big. The mountains ringed it on all sides. The valley was a level bowl, surrounded by dark violet hills. Outside, beyond the hills, the regular world began. Parched fields. Blasted, poverty-stricken towns. Decayed roads. The remains of houses, tumbled-down farm buildings. Ruined cars and machinery. Dust-covered people creeping listlessly around in hand-made clothing, dull rags and tatters.

He had seen the outside. He knew what it was like. At the mountains the blank faces, the disease, the withered crops, the crude plows and ancient tools all ended here. Here, within the ring of hills, Bors had constructed an accurate and detailed reproduction of a society two centuries gone. The world as it had been in the old days. The time of governments. The time that had been pulled down by the Anarchist League.

Within his five synapsis-coils the plans, knowledge, information, blue-prints of a whole world existed. In the two centuries he had carefully recreated that world, had made this miniature society that glittered and hummed on all sides of him. The roads, buildings, houses, industries of a dead world, all a fragment of the past, built with his hands, his own metal fingers and brain.

"Fowler," Bors said.

Fowler came over. He looked haggard. His eyes were red-rimmed and swollen. "What is it? You want to go inside?"

Overhead, the morning patrol thundered past. A string of black dots against the sunny, cloudless sky. Bors watched with satisfaction. "Quite a sight."

"Right on the nose," Fowler agreed, examining his wristwatch. To their right, a column of heavy tanks snaked along a highway between green fields. Their gun-snouts glittered. Behind them a column of foot soldiers marched, faces hidden behind bacteria masks.

"I'm thinking," Bors said, "that it may be unwise to trust Green any longer."

"Why the hell do you say that?"

"Every ten days I'm inactivated. So your crew can see what repairs are needed." Bors twisted restlessly. "For twelve hours I'm completely helpless. Green takes care of me. Sees nothing happens. But --"

"But what?"

"It occurs to me perhaps there'd be more safety in a squad of troops. It's too much of a temptation for one man, alone."

Fowler scowled. "I don't see that. How about me? I have charge of inspecting you. I could switch a few leads around. Send a load through your synapsis-coils. Blow them out."

Bors whirled wildly, then subsided. "True. You could do that." After a moment he demanded, "But what would you gain? You know I'm the only one who can keep all this together. I'm the only one who knows how to maintain a planned society, not a disorderly chaos! If it weren't for me, all this would collapse, and you'd have dust and ruins and weeds. The whole outside would come rushing in to take over!"

"Of course. So why worry about Green?"

Trucks of workers rumbled past. Loads of men in blue-green, sleeves rolled up, armloads of tools. A mining team, heading for the mountains.

"Take me inside," Bors said abruptly.

Fowler called McLean. They hoisted Bors and carried him past the throngs of people, into the building, down the corridor and to his office. Officials and technicians moved respectfully out of the way as the great pitted, corroded tank was carried past.

"All right," Bors said impatiently. "That's all. You can go."

Fowler and McLean left the luxurious office, with its lush carpets, furniture, drapes and rows of books. Bors was already bent over his desk, sorting through heaps of reports and papers.

Fowler shook his head, as they walked down the hall. "He won't last much longer." "The motor system? Can't we reinforce the --"

"I don't mean that. He's breaking up mentally. He can't take the strain any longer." "None of us can," McLean muttered.

"Running this thing is too much for him. Knowing it's all dependent on him. Knowing as soon as he turns his back or lets down it'll begin to come apart at the seams. A hell of a job, trying to shut out the real world. Keeping his model universe running."

"He's gone on a long time," McLean said.

Fowler brooded. "Sooner or later we're going to have to face the situation." Gloomily, he ran his fingers along the blade of a large screwdriver. "He's wearing out. Sooner or later somebody's going to have to step in. As he continues to decay..." He stuck the screwdriver back in his belt, with his pliers and hammer and soldering iron. "One crossed wire."

"What's that?"

Fowler laughed. "Now he's got me doing it. One crossed wire and --poof. But what then? That's the big question."

"Maybe," McLean said softly, "you and I can then get off this rat race. You and I and all the rest of us. And live like human beings."

"Rat race,"Fowler murmured. "Rats in a maze. Doing tricks. Performing chores thought up by somebody else."

McLean caught Fowler's eye. "By somebody of another species."

Tolby struggled vaguely. Silence. A faint dripping close by. A beam pinned his body down. He was caught on all sides by the twisted wreck of the car. He was head down. The car was turned on its side. Off the road in a gully, wedged between two huge trees.

Bent struts and smashed metal all around him. And bodies.

He pushed up with all his strength. The beam gave, and he managed to get to a sitting position. A tree branch had burst in the windshield. The black-haired girl, still turned toward the back seat, was impaled on it. The branch had driven through her spine, out her chest, and into the seat; she clutched at it with both hands, head limp, mouth half-open. The man beside her was also dead. His hands were gone; the windshield had burst around him. He lay in a heap among the remains of the dashboard and the bloody shine of his own internal organs.

Penn was dead. Neck snapped like a rotten broom handle. Tolby pushed his corpse aside and examined his daughter. Silvia didn't stir. He put his ear to her shirt and listened. She was alive. Her heart beat faintly. Her bosom rose and fell against his ear.

He wound a handkerchief around her arm, where the flesh was ripped open and oozing blood. She was badly cut and scratched; one leg was doubled under her, obviously broken. Her clothes were ripped, her hair matted with blood. But she was alive. He pushed the twisted door open and stumbled out. A fiery tongue of afternoon sunlight struck him and he winced. He began to ease her limp body out of the car, past the twisted door-frame.

A sound.

Tolby glanced up, rigid. Something was coming. A whirring insect that rapidly descended. He let go of Silvia, crouched, glanced around, then lumbered awkwardly down the gully. He slid and fell and rolled among the green vines and jagged gray boulders. His gun gripped, he lay gasping in the moist shadows, peering, upward.

The insect landed. A small air-ship, jet-driven. The sight stunned him. He had heard about jets, seen photographs of them. Been briefed and lectured in the history-indoctrination courses at the League Camps. But to see a jet!

Men swarmed out. Uniformed men who started from the road, down the side of the gully, bodies crouched warily as they approached the wrecked car. They lugged heavy rifles. They looked grim and experienced, as they tore the car doors open and scrambled in.

"One's gone," a voice drifted to him.

"Must be around somewhere."

"Look, this one's alive! This woman. Started to crawl out. The rest all dead."

Furious cursing. "Damn Laura! She should have leaped! The fanatic little fool!"

"Maybe she didn't have time. God's sake, the thing's all the way through her." Horror and shocked dismay. "We won't hardly be able to get her loose."

"Leave her." The officer directing things waved the men back out of the car. "Leave them all."

"How about this wounded one?"

The leader hesitated. "Kill her," he said finally. He snatched a rifle and raised the butt. "The rest of you fan out and try to get the other one. He's probably --"

Tolby fired, and the leader's body broke in half. The lower part sank down slowly; the upper dissolved in ashy fragments. Tolby turned and began to move in a slow circle, firing as he crawled. He got two more of them before the rest retreated in panic to their jet-powered insect and slammed the lock.

He had the element of surprise. Now that was gone. They had strength and numbers. He was doomed. Already, the insect was rising. They'd be able to spot him easily from above. But he had saved Silvia. That was something.

He stumbled down a dried-up creek bed. He ran aimlessly; he had no place to go. He didn't know the countryside, and he was on foot. He slipped on a stone and fell headlong. Pain and billowing darkness beat at him as he got unsteadily to his knees. His gun was gone, lost in the shrubbery. He spat broken teeth and blood. He peered wildly up at the blazing afternoon sky.

The insect was leaving. It hummed off toward the distant hills. It dwindled, became a black ball, a fly-speck, then disappeared.

Tolby waited a moment. Then he struggled up the side of the ravine to the wrecked car. They had gone to get help. They'd be back. Now was his only chance. If he could get Silvia out and down the road, into hiding. Maybe to a farmhouse. Back to town.

He reached the car and stood, dazed and stupefied. Three bodies remained, the two in the front seat, Penn in the back. But Silvia was gone.

They had taken her with them. Back where they came from.

She had been dragged to the jet-driven insect; a trail of blood led from the car up the side of the gully to the highway.

With a violent shudder Tolby pulled himself together. He climbed into the car and pried loose Penn's gun from his belt. Silvia's ironite staff rested on the seat; he took that, too. Then he started off down the road, walking without haste, carefully, slowly.

An ironic thought plucked at his mind. He had found what they were after. The men in uniform. They were organized, responsible to a central authority. In a newly-assembled jet.

Beyond the hills was a government.

"Sir," Green said. He smoothed his short blond hair anxiously, his young face twisting.

Technicians and experts and ordinary people in droves were everywhere. The offices buzzed and echoed with the business of the day. Green pushed through the crowd and to the desk where Bors sat, propped up by two magnetic frames.

"Sir," Green said. "Something's happened."

Bors looked up. He pushed a metal-foil slate away and laid down his stylus. His eye cells clicked and flickered; deep inside his battered trunk motor gears whined. "What is it?"

Green came close. There was something in his face, an expression Bors had never seen before. A look of fear and glassy determination. A glazed, fanatic cast, as if his flesh had hardened to rock. "Sir, scouts contacted a League team moving North. They met the team outside Fairfax. The incident took place directly beyond the first road block."

Bors said nothing. On all sides, officials, experts, farmers, workmen, industrial managers, soldiers, people of all kinds buzzed and murmured and pushed forward impatiently. Trying to get to Bors' desk. Loaded down with problems to be solved, situations to be explained. The pressing business of the day. Roads, factories, disease control. Repairs. Construction. Manufacture. Design. Planning. Urgent problems for Bors to consider and deal with. Problems that couldn't wait.

"Was the League team destroyed?" Bors said.

"One was killed. One was wounded and brought here." Green hesitated. "One escaped."

For a long time Bors was silent. Around him the people murmured and shuffled; he ignored them. All at once he pulled the vid-scanner to him and snapped the circuit open. "One escaped? I don't like the sound of that."

"He shot three members of our scout unit. Including the leader. The others got frightened. They grabbed the injured girl and returned here."

Bors' massive head lifted. "They made a mistake. They should have located the one who escaped."

"This was the first time the situation --"

"I know," Bors said. "But it was an error. Better not to have touched them at all, than to have taken two and allowed the third to get away." He turned to the vidscanner. "Sound an emergency alert. Close down the factories. Arm the work crews and any male farmers capable of using weapons. Close every road. Remove the women and children to the undersurface shelters. Bring up the heavy guns and supplies. Suspend all non-military production and --" He considered. "Arrest everyone we're not sure of. On the C sheet. Have them shot." He snapped the scanner off.

"What'll happen?" Green demanded, shaken.

"The thing we've prepared for. Total war."

"We have weapons!" Green shouted excitedly. "In an hour there'll be ten thousand men ready to fight. We have jet-driven ships. Heavy artillery. Bombs. Bacteria pellets. What's the League? A lot of people with packs on their backs!"

"Yes," Bors said. "A lot of people with packs on their backs."

"How can they do anything? How can a bunch of anarchists organize? They have no structure, no control, no central power."

"They have the whole world. A billion people."

"Individuals! A club, not subject to law. Voluntary membership. We have disciplined organization. Every aspect of our economic life operates at maxi-mum efficiency. We—you—have your thumb on everything. All you have to do is give the order. Set the machine in motion."

Bors nodded slowly. "It's true the anarchist can't coordinate. The League can't organize. It's a paradox. Government by anarchists... Anti-government, actually. Instead of governing the world they tramp around to make sure no one else does."

"Dog in the manger."

"As you say, they're actually a voluntary club of totally unorganized individuals. Without law or central authority. They maintain no society—they can't govern. All they can do is interfere with anyone else who tries. Trouble-makers. But --"

"But what?"

"It was this way before. Two centuries ago. They were unorganized. Unarmed. Vast mobs, without discipline or authority. Yet they pulled down all the governments. All over the world."

"We've got a whole army. All the roads are mined. Heavy guns. Bombs. Pellets. Every one of us is a soldier. We're an armed camp!"

Bors was deep in thought. "You say one of them is here? One of the League agents?"

"A young woman."

Bors signaled the nearby maintenance crew. "Take me to her. I want to talk to her in the time remaining."

Silvia watched silently, as the uniformed men pushed and grunted their way into the room. They staggered over to the bed, pulled two chairs together, and carefully laid down their massive armload.

Quickly they snapped protective struts into place, locked the chairs together, threw magnetic grapples into operation, and then warily retreated.

"All right," the robot said. "You can go." The men left. Bors turned to face the woman on the bed.

"A machine," Silvia whispered, white-faced. "You're a machine."

Bors nodded slightly without speaking.

Silvia shifted uneasily on the bed. She was weak. One leg was in a trans-parent plastic cast. Her face was bandaged and her right arm ached and throbbed. Outside the window, the late afternoon sun sprinkled through the drapes. Flowers bloomed. Grass. Hedges. And beyond the hedges, buildings and factories.

For the last hour the sky had been filled with jet-driven ships. Great flocks that raced excitedly across the sky toward distant hills. Along the highway cars hurtled, dragging guns and heavy military equipment. Men were marching in close rank, rows of gray-clad soldiers, guns and helmets and bacteria masks. Endless lines of figures,

BLAIR GAUNTT

identical in their uniforms, stamped from the same matrix.

"There are a lot of them," Bors said, indicating the marching men.

"Yes." Silvia watched a couple of soldiers hurry by the window. Youths with worried expressions on their smooth faces. Helmets bobbing at their waists. Long rifles. Canteens. Counters. Radiation shields. Bacteria masks wound awkwardly around their necks, ready to go into place. They were scared. Hardly more than kids. Others followed. A truck roared into life. The soldiers were swept off to join the others.

"They're going to fight," Bors said, "to defend their homes and factories."

"All this equipment. You manufacture it, don't you?"

"That's right. Our industrial organization is perfect. We're totally productive. Our society here is operated rationally. Scientifically. We're fully prepared to meet this emergency."

Suddenly Silvia realized what the emergency was. "The League! One of us must have got away." She pulled herself up. "Which of them? Penn or my father?"

"I don't know," the robot murmured indifferently.

Horror and disgust choked Silvia. "My God," she said softly. "You have no understanding of us. You run all this, and you're incapable of empathy. You're nothing but a mechanical computer. One of the old government integration robots."

"That's right. Two centuries old."

She was appalled. "And you've been alive all this time. We thought we destroyed all of you!"

"I was missed. I had been damaged. I wasn't in my place. I was in a truck, on my way out of Washington. I saw the mobs and escaped."

"Two hundred years ago. Legendary times. You actually saw the events they tell us about. The old days. The great marches. The day the governments fell."

"Yes. I saw it all. A group of us formed in Virginia. Experts, officials, skilled workmen. Later we came here. It was remote enough, off the beaten path."

"We heard rumors. A fragment... still maintaining itself. But we didn't know where or how."

"I was fortunate," Bors said. "I escaped by a fluke. All the others were destroyed. It's taken a long time to organize what you see here. Fifteen miles from here is a ring of hills. This valley is a bowl—mountains on all sides. We've set up road blocks in the form of natural slides. Nobody comes here. Even in Fairfax, thirty miles off, they know nothing."

"That girl. Laura."

"Scouts. We keep scout teams in all inhabited regions within a hundred mile radius. As soon as you entered Fairfax, word was relayed to us. An air unit was dispatched. To avoid questions, we arranged to have you killed in an auto Wreck. But one of you escaped."

Silvia shook her head, bewildered. "How?" she demanded. "How do you keep going? Don't the people revolt?" She struggled to a sitting position. "They must know what's happened everywhere else. How do you control them? They're going out now, in their uniforms. But—will they fight? Can you count on them?"

Bors answered slowly. "They trust me," he said. "I brought with me a vast amount of knowledge. Information and techniques lost to the rest of the world. Are jet-ships and vidscanners and power cables made anywhere else in the world? I retain all that knowledge. I have memory units, synapsis-coils. Because of me they have these things. Things you know only as dim memories, vague legends."

"What happens when you die?"

"I won't die! I'm eternal!"

"You're wearing out. You have to be carried around. And your right arm. You can hardly move it!" Silvia's voice was harsh, ruthless. "Your whole tank is pitted and rusty."

The robot whirred; for a moment he seemed unable to speak. "My knowledge remains," he grated finally. "I'll always be able to communicate. Fowler has arranged a broadcast system. Even when I talk --" He broke off. "Even then. Everything is under control. I've organized every aspect of the situation. I've maintained this system for two centuries. It's got to be kept going!"

Silvia lashed out. It happened in a split second. The boot of her cast caught the chairs on which the robot rested. She thrust violently with her foot and hands; the chairs teetered, hesitated --

"Fowler!" the robot screamed.

Silvia pushed with all her strength. Blinding agony seared through her leg; she bit her lip and threw her shoulder against the robot's pitted hulk. He waved his arms, whirred wildly, and then the two chairs slowly collapsed. The robot slid quietly from them, over on his back, his arms still waving helplessly.

Silvia dragged herself from the bed. She managed to pull herself to the window; her broken leg hung uselessly, a dead weight in its transparent plastic cast. The robot lay like some futile bug, arms waving, eye lens clicking, its rusty works whirring in fear and rage.

"Fowler!" it screamed again. "Help me!"

Silvia reached the window. She tugged at the locks; they were sealed. She grabbed up a lamp from the table and threw it against the glass. The glass burst around her, a shower of lethal fragments. She stumbled forward—and then the repair crew was pouring into the room.

Fowler gasped at the sight of the robot on its back. A strange expression crossed his face. "Look at him!"

"Help me!" the robot shrilled. "Help me!"

One of the men grabbed Silvia around the waist and lugged her back to the bed. She kicked and bit, sunk her nails into the man's cheek. He threw her on the bed, face down, and drew his pistol. "Stay there," he gasped.

The others were bent over the robot, getting him to an upright position.

"What happened?" Fowler said. He came over to the bed, his face twist-ing. "Did he fall?"

Silvia's eyes glowed with hatred and despair. "I pushed him over. I almost got there." Her chest heaved. "The window. But my leg --"

"Get me back to my quarters!" Bors cried.

The crew gathered him up and carried him down the hall, to his private office. A few moments later he was sitting shakily at his desk, his mechanism pounding wildly, surrounded by his papers and memoranda.

He forced down his panic and tried to resume his work. He had to keep going. His vidscreen was alive with activity. The whole system was in motion. He blankly watched a subcommander sending up a cloud of black dots, jet bombers that shot up like flies and headed quickly off.

The system had to be preserved. He repeated it again and again. He had to save it. Had to organize the people and make them save it. If the people didn't fight, wasn't everything doomed?

Fury and desperation overwhelmed him. The system couldn't preserve itself; it wasn't a thing apart, something that could be separated from the people who lived it. Actually it was the people. They were identical; when the people fought to preserve the system they were fighting to preserve nothing less than themselves.

They existed only as long as the system existed.

He caught sight of a marching column of white-faced troops, moving toward the hills. His ancient synapsis-coils radiated and shuddered uncertainly, then fell back into pattern. He was two centuries old. He had come into existence a long time ago, in a different world. That world had created him; through him that world still lived. As long as he existed, that world existed. In miniature, it still functioned. His model universe, his recreation. His rational, controlled world, in which each aspect was fully organized, fully analyzed and integrated.

He kept a rational, progressive world alive. A humming oasis of productivity on a dusty, parched planet of decay and silence.

Bors spread out his papers and went to work on the most pressing problem. The transformation from a peace-time economy to full military mobilization. Total military organization of every man, woman, child, piece of equipment and dyne of energy under his direction.

Edward Tolby emerged cautiously. His clothes were torn and ragged. He had lost his pack, crawling through the brambles and vines. His face and hands were bleeding. He was utterly exhausted.

Below him lay a valley. A vast bowl. Fields, houses, highways. Factories. Equipment. Men.

He had been watching the men three hours. Endless streams of them, pouring from the valley into the hills, along the roads and paths. On foot, in trucks, in cars, armored tanks, weapons carriers. Overhead, in fast little jet-fighters and great lumbering bombers. Gleaming ships that took up positions above the troops and prepared for battle.

Battle in the grand style. The two-centuries-old full-scale war that was supposed to have disappeared. But here it was, a vision from the past. He had seen this in the old tapes and records, used in the camp orientation courses. A ghost army resurrected to fight again. A vast host of men and guns, prepared to fight and die.

Tolby climbed down cautiously. At the foot of a slope of boulders a soldier had halted his motorcycle and was setting up a communications antenna and transmitter. Tolby circled, crouched, expertly approached him. A blond-haired youth, fumbling nervously with the wires and relays, licking his lips uneasily, glancing up and grabbing for his rifle at every sound

Tolby took a deep breath. The youth had turned his back; he was tracing a power circuit. It was now or never. With one stride Tolby stepped out, raised his pistol and fired. The clump of equipment and the soldier's rifle vanished.

"Don't make a sound," Tolby said. He peered around. No one had seen; the main line was half a mile to his right. The sun was setting. Great shadows were falling over the hills. The fields were rapidly fading from brown-green to a deep violet. "Put your hands up over your head, clasp them, and get down on your knees."

The youth tumbled down in a frightened heap. "What are you going to do?" He saw the ironite staff, and the color left his face. "You're a League agent!"

"Shut up," Tolby ordered. "First, outline your system of responsibility. Who's your superior?"

The youth stuttered forth what he knew. Tolby listened intently. He was satisfied. The usual monolithic structure. Exactly what he wanted.

"At the top," he broke in. "At the top of the pillar. Who has ultimate responsibility?"

"Bors."

"Bors!" Tolby scowled. "That doesn't sound like a name. Sounds like --" He broke off, staggered. "We should have guessed! An old government robot. Still functioning."

The youth saw his chance. He leaped up and darted frantically away.

Tolby shot him above the left ear. The youth pitched over on his face and lay still. Tolby hurried to him and quickly pulled off his dark gray uniform. It was too small for him of course. But the motorcycle was just right. He'd seen tapes of them; he'd wanted one since he was a child. A fast little motorcycle to propel his weight around. Now he had it.

Half an hour later he was roaring down a smooth, broad highway toward the center of the valley and the buildings that rose against the dark sky. His headlights cut into the blackness; he still wobbled from side to side, but for all practical purposes he had the hang of it. He increased speed; the road shot by, trees and fields, haystacks, stalled farm equipment. All traffic was going against him, troops hurrying to the front.

The front. Lemmings going out into the ocean to drown. A thousand, ten thousand, metal-clad figures, armed and alert. Weighted down with guns and bombs and flame throwers and bacteria pellets.

There was only one hitch. No army opposed them. A mistake had been made. It took two sides to make a war, and only one had been resurrected.

A mile outside the concentration of buildings he pulled his motorcycle off the road and carefully hid it in a haystack. For a moment he considered leaving his ironite staff. Then he shrugged and grabbed it up, along with his pistol. He always carried his staff, it was the League symbol. It represented the walking Anarchists who patrolled the world on foot, the world's protection agency.

He loped through the darkness toward the outline ahead. There were fewer men here. He saw no women or children. Ahead, charged wire was set up. Troops crouched behind it, armed to the teeth. A searchlight moved back and forth across the road. Behind it, radar vanes loomed and behind them an ugly square of concrete. The great offices from which the government was run.

For a time he watched the searchlight. Finally he had its motion plotted. In its glare, the faces of the troops stood out, pale and drawn. Youths. They had never fought. This was their first encounter. They were terrified.

When the light was off him, he stood up and advanced toward the wire. Automatically, a breach was slid back for him. Two guards raised up and awkwardly crossed bayonets ahead of him.

"Show your papers!" one demanded. Young lieutenants. Boys, white-lipped, nervous. Playing soldier.

Pity and contempt made Tolby laugh harshly and push forward. "Get out of my way."

One anxiously flashed a pocket light. "Halt! What's the code-key for this watch?" He blocked Tolby's way with his bayonet, hands twisting convulsively.

Tolby reached in his pocket, pulled out his pistol, and as the searchlight started to swerve back, blasted the two guards. The bayonets clattered down and he dived forward. Yells and shapes rose on all sides. Anguished, terrified shouts. Random firing. The night was lit up, as he dashed and crouched, turned a corner past a supply warehouse, raced up a flight of stairs and into the massive building ahead.

He had to work fast. Gripping his ironite staff, he plunged down a gloomy corridor. His boots echoed. Men poured into the building behind him. Bolts of energy thundered past him; a whole section of the ceiling burst into ash and collapsed behind him.

He reached stairs and climbed rapidly. He came to the next floor and groped for the door handle. Something flickered behind him. He half-turned, his gun quickly up --

A stunning blow sent him sprawling. He crashed against the wall; his gun flew from his fingers. A shape bent over him, rifle gripped. "Who are you? What are you doing here?"

Not a soldier. A stubble-chinned man in stained shirt and rumpled trousers. Eyes puffy and red. A belt of tools, hammer, pliers, screwdriver, a soldering iron, around his waist.

Tolby raised himself up painfully. "If you didn't have that rifle --"

Fowler backed warily away. "Who are you? This floor is forbidden to troops of the line. You know this -" Then he saw the ironite staff. "By God," he said softly. "You're the one they didn't get." He laughed shakily. "You're the one who got away."

Tolby's fingers tightened around the staff, but Fowler reacted instantly. The snout of the rifle jerked up, on a line with Tolby's face.

"Be careful," Fowler warned. He turned slightly; soldiers were hurrying up the stairs, boots drumming, echoing shouts ringing. For a moment he hesitated, then waved his rifle toward the stairs ahead.

"Up. Get going."

Toby blinked. "What --"

"Up!" The rifle snout jabbed into Tolby. "Hurry!"

Bewildered, Tolby hurried up the stairs, Fowler close behind him. At the third floor Fowler pushed him roughly through the doorway, the snout of his rifle digging urgently into his back. He found himself in a corridor of doors. Endless offices.

"Keep going," Fowler snarled. "Down the hall. Hurry!"

Tolby hurried, his mind spinning. "What the hell are you --"

"I could never do it," Fowler gasped, close to his ear. "Not in a million years. But it's got to be done."

Tolby halted.

"What is this?"

They faced each other defiantly, faces contorted, eyes blazing. "He's in there," Fowler snapped, indicating a door with his rifle. "You have one chance. Take it."

For a fraction of a second Tolby hesitated. Then he broke away. "Okay. I'll take it."

Fowler followed after him. "Be careful. Watch your step. There's a series of check points. Keep going straight, in all the way. As far as you can go. And for God's sake, hurry!"

His voice faded, as Tolby gained speed. He reached the door and tore it open.

Soldiers and officials ballooned. He threw himself against them; they sprawled and scattered. He scrambled on, as they struggled up and stupidly fumbled for their guns. Through another door, into an inner office, past a desk where a frightened girl sat, eyes wide, mouth open. Then a third door, into an alcove.

A wild-faced youth leaped up and snatched frantically for his pistol. Tolby was unarmed, trapped in the alcove. Figures already pushed against the door behind him. He gripped his ironite staff and backed away as the blond-haired fanatic fired blindly. The bolt burst a foot away; it flicked him with a tongue of heat.

"You dirty anarchist!" Green screamed. His face distorted, he fired again and again. "You murdering anarchist spy!"

Tolby hurled his ironite staff. He put all his strength in it; the staff leaped through the air in a whistling arc, straight at the youth's head. Green saw it coming and ducked. Agile and quick, he jumped away, grinning humorlessly. The staff crashed against the wall and rolled clanging to the floor.

"Your walking staff!" Green gasped and fired.

The bolt missed him on purpose. Green was playing games with him. Tolby bent down and groped frantically for the staff. He picked it up. Green watched, face rigid, eyes glittering. "Throw it again!" he snarled.

Tolby leaped. He took the youth by surprise. Green grunted, stumbled back from the impact, then suddenly fought with maniacal fury.

Tolby was heavier. But he was exhausted. He had crawled hours, beat his way through the mountains, walked endlessly. He was at the end of his strength. The car wreck, the days of walking. Green was in perfect shape. His wiry, agile body twisted away. His hands came up. Fingers dug into Tolby's windpipe; he kicked the youth in the groin. Green staggered back, convulsed and bent over with pain.

"All right," Green gasped, face ugly and dark. His hand fumbled with his pistol. The barrel came up.

Half of Green's head dissolved. His hands opened and his gun fell to the floor. His body stood for a moment, then settled down in a heap, like an empty suit of clothes.

Tolby caught a glimpse of a rifle snout pushed past him—and the man with the tool belt. The man waved him on frantically. "Hurry!"

Tolby raced down a carpeted hall, between two great flickering yellow lamps. A crowd of officials and soldiers stumbled uncertainly after him, shouting and firing at random. He tore open a thick oak door and halted.

He was in a luxurious chamber. Drapes, rich wallpaper. Lamps. Book-cases. A glimpse of the finery of the past. The wealth of the old days. Thick carpets. Warm radiant heat. A vidscreen. At the far end, a huge mahogany desk.

At the desk a figure sat. Working on heaps of papers and reports, piled masses of material. The figure contrasted starkly with the lushness of the furnishings. It was a great pitted, corroded tank of metal. Bent and greenish, patched and repaired. An ancient machine.

"Is that you, Fowler?" the robot demanded.

Tolby advanced, his ironite staff gripped.

The robot turned angrily. "Who is it? Get Green and carry me down into the shelter. One of the roadblocks has reported a League agent already --" The robot broke off. Its cold, mechanical eye lens bored up at the man. It clicked and whirred in uneasy astonishment. "I don't know you."

It saw the ironite staff.

"League agent," the robot said. "You're the one who got through." Com-prehension came."The third one. You came here. You didn't go back." Its metal fingers fumbled clumsily at the objects on the desk, then in the drawer. It found a gun and raised it awkwardly.

Tolby knocked the gun away; it clattered to the floor.

"Run!" he shouted at the robot. "Start running!"

It remained. Tolby's staff came down. The fragile, complex brain-unit of the robot burst apart. Coils, wiring, relay fluid, spattered over his arms and hands. The robot shuddered. Its machinery thrashed. It half-rose from its chair, then swayed and toppled. It crashed full length on the floor, parts and gears rolling in all directions.

"Good God," Tolby said, suddenly seeing it for the first time. Shakily, he bent over its remains. "It was crippled."

Men were all around him. "He's killed Bors!" Shocked, dazed faces. "Bors is dead!"

Fowler came up slowly. "You got him, all right. There's nothing left now."

Tolby stood holding his ironite staff in his hands. "The poor blasted thing," he said softly. "Completely helpless. Sitting there and I came and killed him. He didn't have a chance."

The building was bedlam. Soldiers and officials scurried crazily about, grief-stricken, hysterical.

They bumped into each other, gathered in knots, shouted and gave meaningless orders.

Tolby pushed past them; nobody paid any attention to him. Fowler was gathering up the remains of the robot. Collecting the smashed pieces and bits. Tolby stopped beside him. Like Humpty-Dumpty, pulled down off his wall he'd never be back together, not now.

"Where's the woman?" he asked Fowler. "The League agent they brought in."

Fowler straightened up slowly. "I'll take you." He led Tolby down the packed, surging hall, to the hospital wing of the building.

Silvia sat up apprehensively as the two men entered the room. "What's going on?" She recognized her father. "Dad! Thank God! It was you who got out."

Tolby slammed the door against the chaos of sound hammering up and down the corridor. "How are you? How's your leg?"

"Mending. What happened?"

"I got him. The robot. He's dead."

For a moment the three of them were silent. Outside, in the halls, men ran frantically back and forth. Word had already leaked out. Troops gathered in huddled knots outside the building. Lost men, wandering away from their posts. Uncertain. Aimless.

"It's over," Fowler said.

Tolby nodded. "I know."

"They'll get tired of crouching in their foxholes," Fowler said. "They'll come filtering back. As soon as the news reaches them, they'll desert and throw away their equipment."

"Good," Tolby grunted. "The sooner the better." He touched Fowler's rifle. "You, too, I hope." Silvia hesitated. "Do you think --"

"Think what?"

"Did we make a mistake?"

Tolby grinned wearily. "Hell of a time to think about that."

"He was doing what he thought was right. They built up their homes and factories. This whole area... They turn out a lot of goods. I've been watching through the window. It's made me think. They've done so much. Made so much."

"Made a lot of guns," Tolby said.

"We have guns, too. We kill and destroy. We have all the disadvantages and none of the advantages."

"We don't have war," Tolby answered quietly. "To defend this neat little organization there are ten thousand men up there in those hills. All waiting to fight. Waiting to drop their bombs and bacteria pellets, to keep this place running. But they won't. Pretty soon they'll give up and start to trickle back."

"This whole system will decay rapidly," Fowler said. "He was already losing his control. He couldn't keep the clock back much longer."

"Anyhow, it's done," Silvia murmured. "We did our job." She smiled a little. "Bors did his job and we did ours. But the times were against him and with us."

"That's right," Tolby agreed. "We did our job. And we'll never be sorry."

Fowler said nothing. He stood with his hands in his pockets, gazing silently out the window. His fingers were touching something. Three undamaged synapsis-coils. Intact memory elements from the dead robot, snatched from the scattered remains.

Just in case, he said to himself. Just in case the times change.

Edward Morgan Forster *(1879–1970) was most famous for his novels about class issues in the British Empire, like Howard's End and A Room with a View. The Machine Stops was Forster's only forray into science fiction and first published in the Oxford and Cambridge Review in 1909.*

THE MACHINE STOPS

by E.M. Forster

THE AIR-SHIP

Imagine, if you can, a small room, hexagonal in shape, like the cell of a bee. It is lighted neither by window nor by lamp, yet it is filled with a soft radiance. There are no apertures for ventilation, yet the air is fresh. There are no musical instruments, and yet, at the moment that my meditation opens, this room is throbbing with melodious sounds. An armchair is in the centre, by its side a read-ing-desk—that is all the furniture. And in the armchair there sits a swaddled lump of flesh—a woman, about five feet high, with a face as white as a fungus. It is to her that the little room belongs.

An electric bell rang.

The woman touched a switch and the music was silent.

"I suppose I must see who it is", she thought, and set her chair in motion. The chair, like the music, was worked by machinery and it rolled her to the other side of the room where the bell still rang importunately.

"Who is it?" she called. Her voice was irritable, for she had been interrupted often since the music began. She knew several thousand people, in certain directions human intercourse had ad-vanced enormously.

But when she listened into the receiver, her white face wrin-kled into smiles, and she said:

"Very well. Let us talk, I will isolate myself. I do not expect anything important will happen for the next five minutes—for I can give you fully five minutes, Kuno. Then I must deliver my lecture on 'Music during the

Australian Period'."

She touched the isolation knob, so that no one else could speak to her. Then she touched the lighting apparatus, and the little room was plunged into darkness.

"Be quick!" She called, her irritation returning. "Be quick, Kuno; here I am in the dark wasting my time."

But it was fully fifteen seconds before the round plate that she held in her hands began to glow. A faint blue light shot across it, darkening to purple, and presently she could see the image of her son, who lived on the other side of the earth, and he could see her.

"Kuno, how slow you are."

He smiled gravely.

"I really believe you enjoy dawdling."

"I have called you before, mother, but you were always busy or isolated. I have something particular to say."

"What is it, dearest boy? Be quick. Why could you not send it by pneumatic post?"

"Because I prefer saying such a thing. I want--"

"Well?"

"I want you to come and see me."

Vashti watched his face in the blue plate.

"But I can see you!" she exclaimed. "What more do you want?"

"I want to see you not through the Machine," said Kuno. "I want to speak to you not through the wearisome Machine."

"Oh, hush!" said his mother, vaguely shocked. "You mustn't say anything against the Machine." "Why not?"

"One mustn't."

"You talk as if a god had made the Machine," cried the other. "I believe that you pray to it when you are unhappy. Men made it, do not forget that. Great men, but men. The Machine is much, but it is not everything. I see something like you in this plate, but I do not see you. I hear something like you through this telephone, but I do not hear you. That is why I want you to come. Pay me a visit, so that we can meet face to face, and talk about the hopes that are in my mind."

She replied that she could scarcely spare the time for a visit. "The air-ship barely takes two days to fly between me and you." "I dislike air-ships."

"Why?"

"I dislike seeing the horrible brown earth, and the sea, and the stars when it is dark. I get no ideas in an air-ship."

"I do not get them anywhere else."

"What kind of ideas can the air give you?"

He paused for an instant.

"Do you not know four big stars that form an oblong, and three stars close together in the middle of the oblong, and hanging from these stars, three other stars?"

"No, I do not. I dislike the stars. But did they give you an idea? How interesting; tell me." "I had an idea that they were like a man."

"I do not understand."

"The four big stars are the man's shoulders and his knees.

The three stars in the middle are like the belts that men wore once, and the three stars hanging are like a sword."

"A sword?;"

"Men carried swords about with them, to kill animals and other men."

"It does not strike me as a very good idea, but it is certainly original. When did it come to you first?"

"In the air-ship---" He broke off, and she fancied that he looked sad. She could not be sure, for the Machine did not transmit nuances of expression. It only gave a general idea of people—an idea that was good enough for all practical purposes, Vashti thought. The imponderable bloom, declared by a discredited philosophy to be the actual essence of intercourse, was rightly ignored by the Machine, just as the imponderable bloom of the grape was ignored by the manufacturers of artificial fruit. Something "good enough" had long since been accepted by our race.

"The truth is," he continued, "that I want to see these stars again. They are curious stars. I want to see them not from the air-ship, but from the surface of the earth, as our ancestors did, thousands of years ago. I want to visit the surface of the earth."

She was shocked again.

"Mother, you must come, if only to explain to me what is the harm of visiting the surface of the earth."

"No harm," she replied, controlling herself. "But no advantage. The surface of the earth is only dust and mud, no advantage. The surface of the earth is only dust and mud, no life remains on it, and you would need a respirator, or the cold of the outer air would kill you. One dies immediately in the outer air."

"I know; of course I shall take all precautions."

"And besides--" "Well?"

She considered, and chose her words with care. Her son had a queer temper, and she wished to dissuade him from the expedition.

"It is contrary to the spirit of the age," she asserted. "Do you mean by that, contrary to the Machine?" "In a sense, but--"

His image is the blue plate faded.

"Kuno!"

He had isolated himself. For a moment Vashti felt lonely.

Then she generated the light, and the sight of her room, flooded with radiance and studded with electric buttons, revived her. There were buttons and switches everywhere—buttons to call for food for music, for clothing. There was the hot-bath button, by pressure of which a basin of (imitation) marble rose out of the floor, filled to the brim with a warm deodorized liquid. There was the cold-bath button. There was the button that produced literature, and there were of course the buttons by which she communicated with her friends. The room, though it contained nothing, was in touch with all that she cared for in the world.

Vashanti's next move was to turn off the isolation switch, and all the accumulations of the last three minutes burst upon her. The room was filled with the noise of bells, and speaking-tubes. What was the new food like? Could she recommend it? Has she had any ideas lately? Might one tell her one's own ideas? Would she make an engagement to visit the public nurseries at an early date?--say this day month.

To most of these questions she replied with irritation—a growing quality in that accelerated age. She said that the new food was horrible. That she could not visit the public nurseries through press of engagements. That she had no ideas of her own but had just been told one—that four stars and three in the middle were like a man: she doubted there was much in it. Then she switched off her correspondents, for it was time to deliver her lecture on Australian music.

The clumsy system of public gatherings had been long since abandoned; neither Vashti nor her audience stirred from their rooms. Seated in her armchair she spoke, while they in their armchairs heard her, fairly well, and saw her, fairly well. She opened with a humorous account of music in the pre Mongolian epoch, and went on to describe the great outburst of song that followed the Chinese conquest. Remote and prim¾val as were the methods of I-San-So and the Brisbane school, she yet felt (she said) that study of them might repay the musicians of today: they had freshness; they had, above all, ideas. Her lecture, which lasted ten minutes, was well received, and at its conclusion she and many of her audience listened to a lecture on the sea; there were ideas to be got from the sea; the speaker had donned a respirator and visited it lately. Then she fed, talked to many friends, had a bath, talked again, and summoned her bed.

The bed was not to her liking. It was too large, and she had a feeling for a small bed. Complaint was useless, for beds were of the same dimension all over the world, and to have had an alternative size would have involved vast alterations in the Machine. Vashti isolated herself—it was necessary, for neither day nor night existed under the ground—and reviewed all that had happened since she had summoned the bed last. Ideas? Scarcely any. Events—was Kuno's invitation an event?

By her side, on the little reading-desk, was a survival from the ages of litter—one book. This was the Book of the Machine. In it were instructions against every possible contingency. If she was hot or cold or dyspeptic or at a loss for a word, she went to the book, and it told her which button to press. The Central Committee published it. In accordance with a growing habit, it was richly bound.

Sitting up in the bed, she took it reverently in her hands. She glanced round the glowing room as if some one might be watching her. Then, half ashamed, half joyful, she murmured "O Machine!" and raised the volume to her lips. Thrice she kissed it, thrice inclined her head, thrice she felt the delirium of acquiescence. Her ritual performed, she turned to page 1367, which gave the times of the departure of the air-ships from the island in the southern hemisphere, under whose soil she lived, to the island in the northern hemisphere, whereunder lived her son.

She thought, "I have not the time."

She made the room dark and slept; she awoke and made the room light; she ate and exchanged ideas with her friends, and listened to music and attended lectures; she make the room dark and slept. Above her, beneath her, and around her, the Machine hummed eternally; she did not notice the noise, for she had been born with it in her ears. The earth, carrying her, hummed as it sped through silence, turning her now to the invisible sun, now to the invisible stars. She awoke and made the room light.

"Kuno!"

"I will not talk to you." he answered, "until you come."

"Have you been on the surface of the earth since we spoke last?" His image faded.

Again she consulted the book. She became very nervous and lay back in her chair palpitating. Think of her as without teeth or hair. Presently she directed the chair to the wall, and pressed an unfamiliar button. The wall swung apart slowly. Through the opening she saw a tunnel that curved slightly, so that its goal was not visible. Should she go to see her son, here was the beginning of the journey.

Of course she knew all about the communication-system. There was nothing mysterious in it. She would summon a car and it would fly with her down the tunnel until it reached the lift that communicated with the air-ship station: the system had been in use for many, many years, long before the universal establishment of the Machine. And of course she had studied the civilization that had immediately preceded her own—the civilization that had mistaken the functions of the system, and had used it for bringing people to things, instead of for bringing things to people. Those funny old days, when men went for change of air instead of changing the air in their rooms! And yet—she was frightened of the tunnel: she had not seen it since her last child was born. It curved—but not quite as she remembered; it was brilliant—but not quite as brilliant as a lecturer had suggested. Vashti was seized with the terrors of direct experience. She shrank back into the room, and the wall closed up again.

"Kuno," she said, "I cannot come to see you. I am not well."

Immediately an enormous apparatus fell on to her out of the ceiling, a thermometer was automatically laid upon her heart. She lay powerless. Cool pads soothed her forehead. Kuno had telegraphed to her doctor.

So the human passions still blundered up and down in the Machine. Vashti drank the medicine that the doctor projected into her mouth, and the machinery retired into the ceiling. The voice of Kuno was heard asking how she felt.

"Better." Then with irritation: "But why do you not come to me instead?" "Because I cannot leave this place."

"Why?"

"Because, any moment, something tremendous many happen."

"Have you been on the surface of the earth yet?" "Not yet."

"Then what is it?"

"I will not tell you through the Machine."

She resumed her life.

But she thought of Kuno as a baby, his birth, his removal to the public nurseries, her own visit to him there, his visits to her—visits which stopped when the Machine had assigned him a room on the other side of the earth. "Parents, duties of," said the book of the Machine," cease at the moment of birth. P.422327483." True, but there was something special about Kuno—indeed there had been something special about all her children—and, after all, she must brave the journey if he desired it. And "something tremendous might happen". What did that mean? The nonsense of a youthful man, no doubt, but she must go. Again she pressed the unfamiliar button, again the wall swung back, and she saw the tunnel that curves out of sight. Clasping the Book, she rose, tottered on to the platform, and summoned the car. Her room closed behind her: the journey to the northern hemisphere had begun.

Of course it was perfectly easy. The car approached and in it she found armchairs exactly like her own. When she signaled, it stopped, and she tottered into the lift. One other passenger was in the lift, the first fellow creature she had seen face to face for months. Few travelled in these days, for, thanks to the advance of science, the earth was exactly alike all over. Rapid intercourse, from which the previous civilization had hoped so much, had ended by defeating itself. What was the good of going to Peking when it was just like Shrewsbury? Why return to Shrewsbury when it would all be like Peking? Men seldom moved their bodies; all unrest was concentrated in the soul.

The air-ship service was a relic form the former age. It was kept up, because it was easier to keep it up than to stop it or to diminish it, but it now far exceeded the wants of the population. Vessel after vessel would rise form the vomitories of Rye or of Christchurch (I use the antique names), would sail into the crowded sky, and would draw up at the wharves of the south—empty, so nicely adjusted was the system, so independent of meteorology, that the sky, whether calm or cloudy, resembled a vast kaleidoscope whereon the same patterns periodically recurred. The ship on which Vashti sailed started now at sunset, now at dawn. But always, as it passed above Rheas, it would neighbour the ship that served between Helsingfors and the Brazils, and, every third time it surmounted the Alps, the fleet of Palermo would cross its track behind. Night and day, wind and storm, tide and earthquake, impeded man no longer. He had harnessed Leviathan. All the old literature, with its praise of Nature, and its fear of Nature, rang false as the prattle of a child.

Yet as Vashti saw the vast flank of the ship, stained with exposure to the outer air, her horror of direct

experience returned. It was not quite like the air-ship in the cinematophote. For one thing it smelt—not strongly or unpleasantly, but it did smell, and with her eyes shut she should have known that a new thing was close to her. Then she had to walk to it from the lift, had to submit to glances form the other passengers. The man in front dropped his Book—no great matter, but it disquieted them all. In the rooms, if the Book was dropped, the floor raised it mechanically, but the gangway to the air-ship was not so prepared, and the sacred volume lay motionless. They stopped—the thing was unforeseen— and the man, instead of picking up his property, felt the muscles of his arm to see how they had failed him. Then some one actually said with direct utterance: "We shall be late"--and they trooped on board, Vashti treading on the pages as she did so.

Inside, her anxiety increased. The arrangements were old-fashioned and rough. There was even a female attendant, to whom she would have to announce her wants during the voyage. Of course a revolving platform ran the length of the boat, but she was expected to walk from it to her cabin. Some cabins were better than others, and she did not get the best. She thought the attendant had been unfair, and spasms of rage shook her. The glass valves had closed, she could not go back. She saw, at the end of the vestibule, the lift in which she had ascended going quietly up and down, empty. Beneath those corridors of shining tiles were rooms, tier below tier, reaching far into the earth, and in each room there sat a human being, eating, or sleeping, or producing ideas. And buried deep in the hive was her own room. Vashti was afraid.

"O Machine!" she murmured, and caressed her Book, and was comforted.

Then the sides of the vestibule seemed to melt together, as do the passages that we see in dreams, the lift vanished, the Book that had been dropped slid to the left and vanished, polished tiles rushed by like a stream of water, there was a slight jar, and the air-ship, issuing from its tunnel, soared above the waters of a tropical ocean.

It was night. For a moment she saw the coast of Sumatra edged by the phosphorescence of waves, and crowned by lighthouses, still sending forth their disregarded beams. These also vanished, and only the stars distracted her. They were not motionless, but swayed to and fro above her head, thronging out of one sky-light into another, as if the universe and not the air-ship was careening. And, as often happens on clear nights, they seemed now to be in perspective, now on a plane; now piled tier beyond tier into the infinite heavens, now concealing infinity, a roof limiting for ever the visions of men. In either case they seemed intolerable. "Are we to travel in the dark?" called the passengers angrily, and the attendant, who had been careless, generated the light, and pulled down the blinds of pliable metal. When the air-ships had been built, the desire to look direct at things still lingered in the world. Hence the extraordinary number of skylights and windows, and the proportionate discomfort to those who were civilized and refined. Even in Vashti's cabin one star peeped through a flaw in the blind, and after a few hers" uneasy slumber, she was disturbed by an unfamiliar glow, which was the dawn.

Quick as the ship had sped westwards, the earth had rolled eastwards quicker still, and had dragged back Vashti and her companions towards the sun. Science could prolong the night, but only for a little, and those high hopes of neutralizing the earth's diurnal revolution had passed, together with hopes that were possibly higher. To "keep pace with the sun," or even to outstrip it, had been the aim of the civilization preceding this. Racing aeroplanes had been built for the purpose, capable of enormous speed, and steered by the greatest intellects of the epoch. Round the globe they went, round and round, westward, westward, round and round, amidst humanity's applause. In vain. The globe went eastward quicker still, horrible accidents occurred, and the Committee of the Machine, at the time rising into prominence, declared the pursuit illegal, unmechanical, and punishable by Homelessness.

Of Homelessness more will be said later.

Doubtless the Committee was right. Yet the attempt to "defeat the sun" aroused the last common interest that our race experienced about the heavenly bodies, or indeed about anything. It was the last time that men were

compacted by thinking of a power outside the world. The sun had conquered, yet it was the end of his spiritual dominion. Dawn, midday, twilight, the zodiacal path, touched neither men's lives not their hearts, and science retreated into the ground, to concentrate herself upon problems that she was certain of solving.

So when Vashti found her cabin invaded by a rosy finger of light, she was annoyed, and tried to adjust the blind. But the blind flew up altogether, and she saw through the skylight small pink clouds, swaying against a background of blue, and as the sun crept higher, its radiance entered direct, brimming down the wall, like a golden sea. It rose and fell with the air-ship's motion, just as waves rise and fall, but it advanced steadily, as a tide advances. Unless she was careful, it would strike her face. A spasm of horror shook her and she rang for the attendant. The attendant too was horrified, but she could do nothing; it was not her place to mend the blind. She could only suggest that the lady should change her cabin, which she accordingly prepared to do.

People were almost exactly alike all over the world, but the attendant of the air-ship, perhaps owing to her exceptional duties, had grown a little out of the common. She had often to address passengers with direct speech, and this had given her a certain roughness and originality of manner. When Vashti served away form the sunbeams with a cry, she behaved barbarically—she put out her hand to steady her.

"How dare you!" exclaimed the passenger. "You forget yourself!"

The woman was confused, and apologized for not having let her fall. People never touched one another. The custom had become obsolete, owing to the Machine.

"Where are we now?" asked Vashti haughtily.

"We are over Asia," said the attendant, anxious to be polite.

"Asia?"

"You must excuse my common way of speaking. I have got into the habit of calling places over which I pass by their unmechanical names."

"Oh, I remember Asia. The Mongols came from it."

"Beneath us, in the open air, stood a city that was once called Simla."

"Have you ever heard of the Mongols and of the Brisbane school?"

"No."

"Brisbane also stood in the open air."

"Those mountains to the right—let me show you them." She pushed back a metal blind. The main chain of the Himalayas was revealed. "They were once called the Roof of the World, those mountains."

"You must remember that, before the dawn of civilization, they seemed to be an impenetrable wall that touched the stars. It was supposed that no one but the gods could exist above their summits. How we have advanced, thanks to the Machine!"

"How we have advanced, thanks to the Machine!" said Vashti.

"How we have advanced, thanks to the Machine!" echoed the passenger who had dropped his Book the night before, and who was standing in the passage.

"And that white stuff in the cracks?--what is it?"

"I have forgotten its name."

"Cover the window, please. These mountains give me no ideas."

The northern aspect of the Himalayas was in deep shadow: on the Indian slope the sun had just prevailed. The forests had been destroyed during the literature epoch for the purpose of making newspaper-pulp, but the snows were awakening to their morning glory, and clouds still hung on the breasts of Kinchinjunga. In the plain were seen the ruins of cities, with diminished rivers creeping by their walls, and by the sides of these were sometimes the signs of vomitories, marking the cities of to day. Over the whole prospect air-ships rushed, crossing the inter-crossing with incredible aplomb, and rising nonchalantly when they desired to escape the perturbations of the lower atmosphere and to traverse the Roof of the World.

"We have indeed advance, thanks to the Machine," repeated the attendant, and his the Himalayas behind a metal blind.

The day dragged wearily forward. The passengers sat each in his cabin, avoiding one another with an almost physical repulsion and longing to be once more under the surface of the earth. There were eight or ten of them, mostly young males, sent out from the public nurseries to inhabit the rooms of those who had died in various parts of the earth. The man who had dropped his Book was on the homeward journey. He had been sent to Sumatra for the purpose of propagating the race. Vashti alone was traveling by her private will.

At midday she took a second glance at the earth. The air-ship was crossing another range of mountains, but she could see little, owing to clouds. Masses of black rock hovered below her, and merged indistinctly into grey. Their shapes were fantastic; one of them resembled a prostrate man.

"No ideas here," murmured Vashti, and hid the Caucasus behind a metal blind.

In the evening she looked again. They were crossing a golden sea, in which lay many small islands and one peninsula. She repeated, "No ideas here," and his Greece behind a metal blind.

II
THE MENDING APPARATUS

By a vestibule, by a lift, by a tubular railway, by a platform, by a sliding door—by reversing all the steps of her departure did Vashti arrive at her son's room, which exactly resembled her own. She might well declare that the visit was superfluous. The buttons, the knobs, the reading-desk with the Book, the temperature, the atmosphere, the illumination—all were exactly the same. And if Kuno himself, flesh of her flesh, stood close beside her at last, what profit was there in that? She was too well-bred to shake him by the hand.

Averting her eyes, she spoke as follows:

"Here I am. I have had the most terrible journey and greatly retarded the development of my soul. It is not worth it, Kuno, it is not worth it. My time is too precious. The sunlight almost touched me, and I have met with the rudest people. I can only stop a few minutes. Say what you want to say, and then I must return."

"I have been threatened with Homelessness," said Kuno. She looked at him now.

"I have been threatened with Homelessness, and I could not tell you such a thing through the Machine." Homelessness means death. The victim is exposed to the air, which kills him.

"I have been outside since I spoke to you last. The tremendous thing has happened, and they have discovered me."

"But why shouldn't you go outside?" she exclaimed, "It is perfectly legal, perfectly mechanical, to visit the surface of the earth. I have lately been to a lecture on the sea; there is no objection to that; one simply summons a respirator and gets an Egression-permit. It is not the kind of thing that spiritually minded people do, and I begged you not to do it, but there is no legal objection to it."

"I did not get an Egression-permit." "Then how did you get out?"

"I found out a way of my own."

The phrase conveyed no meaning to her, and he had to repeat it.

"A way of your own?" she whispered. "But that would be wrong." "Why?"

The question shocked her beyond measure. "You are beginning to worship the Machine," he said coldly.

"You think it irreligious of me to have found out a way of my own. It was just what the Committee thought, when they threatened me with Homelessness."

At this she grew angry. "I worship nothing!" she cried. "I am most advanced. I don't think you irreligious, for there is no such thing as religion left. All the fear and the superstition that existed once have been destroyed by the Machine. I only meant that to find out a way of your own was—Besides, there is no new way out."

"So it is always supposed."

"Except through the vomitories, for which one must have an Egression-permit, it is impossible to get out. The Book says so."

"Well, the Book's wrong, for I have been out on my feet." For Kuno was possessed of a certain physical strength.

By these days it was a demerit to be muscular. Each infant was examined at birth, and all who promised undue strength were destroyed. Humanitarians may protest, but it would have been no true kindness to let an athlete live; he would never have been happy in that state of life to which the Machine had called him; he would have yearned for trees to climb, rivers to bathe in, meadows and hills against which he might measure his body. Man must be adapted to his surroundings, must he not? In the dawn of the world our weakly must be exposed on Mount Taygetus, in its twilight our strong will suffer euthanasia, that the Machine may progress, that the Machine may progress, that the Machine may progress eternally.

"You know that we have lost the sense of space. We say 'space is annihilated', but we have annihilated not space, but the sense thereof. We have lost a part of ourselves. I determined to recover it, and I began by walking up and down the platform of the railway outside my room. Up and down, until I was tired, and so did recapture the meaning of 'Near' and 'Far'. 'Near' is a place to which I can get quickly on my feet, not a place to which the train or the air-ship will take me quickly. 'Far' is a place to which I cannot get quickly on my feet; the vomitory is 'far', though I could be there in thirty-eight seconds by summoning the train. Man is the measure. That was my first lesson. Man's feet are the measure for distance, his hands are the measure for ownership, his body is the measure for all that is lovable and desirable and strong. Then I went further: it was then that I called to you for the first time, and you would not come.

"This city, as you know, is built deep beneath the surface of the earth, with only the vomitories protruding. Having paced the platform outside my own room, I took the lift to the next platform and paced that also, and so with each in turn, until I came to the topmost, above which begins the earth. All the platforms were exactly alike, and all that I gained by visiting them was to develop my sense of space and my muscles. I think I should have been content with this—it is not a little thing,--but as I walked and brooded, it occurred to me that our cities had been built in the days when men still breathed the outer air, and that there had been ventilation shafts for the workmen. I could think of nothing but these ventilation shafts. Had they been destroyed by all the food-tubes and medicine-tubes and music-tubes that the Machine has evolved lately? Or did traces of them remain? One thing was certain. If I came upon them anywhere, it would be in the railway-tunnels of the topmost story. Everywhere else, all space was accounted for.

"I am telling my story quickly, but don't think that I was not a coward or that your answers never depressed me. It is not the proper thing, it is not mechanical, it is not decent to walk along a railway-tunnel. I did not fear that I might tread upon a live rail and be killed. I feared something far more intangible—doing what was not contemplated by the Machine. Then I said to myself, 'Man is the measure', and I went, and after many visits I found an opening.

"The tunnels, of course, were lighted. Everything is light, artificial light; darkness is the exception. So when I saw a black gap in the tiles, I knew that it was an exception, and rejoiced. I put in my arm—I could put in no more at first—and waved it round and round in ecstasy. I loosened another tile, and put in my head, and shouted into the darkness: 'I am coming, I shall do it yet,' and my voice reverberated down endless passages. I seemed to hear the spirits of those dead workmen who had returned each evening to the starlight and to their wives, and all the generations who had lived in the open air called back to me, 'You will do it yet, you are coming,'"

He paused, and, absurd as he was, his last words moved her.

For Kuno had lately asked to be a father, and his request had been refused by the Committee. His was not a type that the Machine desired to hand on.

"Then a train passed. It brushed by me, but I thrust my head and arms into the hole. I had done enough for one day, so I crawled back to the platform, went down in the lift, and summoned my bed. Ah what dreams! And again I called you, and again you refused."

She shook her head and said:

"Don't. Don't talk of these terrible things. You make me miserable. You are throwing civilization away."

"But I had got back the sense of space and a man cannot rest then. I determined to get in at the hole and climb the shaft. And so I exercised my arms. Day after day I went through ridiculous movements, until my flesh ached, and I could hang by my hands and hold the pillow of my bed outstretched for many minutes. Then I summoned a respirator, and started.

"It was easy at first. The mortar had somehow rotted, and I

soon pushed some more tiles in, and clambered after them into the darkness, and the spirits of the dead comforted me. I don't know what I mean by that. I just say what I felt. I felt, for the first time, that a protest had been lodged against corruption, and that even as the dead were comforting me, so I was comforting the unborn. I felt that humanity existed, and that it existed without clothes. How can I possibly explain this? It was naked, humanity seemed naked, and all these tubes and buttons and machineries neither came into the world with us, nor will they follow us out, nor do they matter supremely while we are here. Had I been strong, I would have torn off every garment I had, and gone out into the outer air unswaddled. But this is not for me, nor perhaps for my generation. I climbed with my respirator and my hygienic clothes and my dietetic tabloids! Better thus than not at all.

"There was a ladder, made of some prim3⁄4val metal. The light from the railway fell upon its lowest rungs, and I saw that it led straight upwards out of the rubble at the bottom of the shaft. Perhaps our ancestors ran up and down it a dozen times daily, in their building. As I climbed, the rough edges cut through my gloves so that my hands bled. The light helped me for a little, and then came darkness and, worse still, silence which pierced my ears like a sword. The Machine hums! Did you know that? Its hum penetrates our blood, and may even guide our thoughts. Who knows! I was getting beyond its power. Then I thought: 'This silence means that I am doing wrong.' But I heard voices in the silence, and again they strengthened me." He laughed. "I had need of them. The next moment I cracked my head against something."

She sighed.

"I had reached one of those pneumatic stoppers that defend us from the outer air. You may have noticed them no the air-ship. Pitch dark, my feet on the rungs of an invisible ladder, my hands cut; I cannot explain how I lived through this part, but the voices till comforted me, and I felt for fastenings. The stopper, I suppose, was about eight feet across. I passed my hand over it as far as I could reach. It was perfectly smooth. I felt it almost to the centre. Not quite to the centre, for my arm was too short. Then the voice said: 'Jump. It is worth it. There may be a handle in the centre, and you may catch hold of it and so come to us your own way. And if there is no handle, so that you may fall and are dashed to pieces—it is till worth it: you will still come to us your own way.' So I jumped. There was a handle, and --"

He paused. Tears gathered in his mother's eyes. She knew that he was fated. If he did not die today he would die tomorrow. There was not room for such a person in the world. And with her pity disgust mingled. She was ashamed at having borne such a son, she who had always been so respectable and so full of ideas. Was he really the little boy to whom she had taught the use of his stops and buttons, and to whom she had given his first lessons in the Book? The very hair that disfigured his lip showed that he was reverting to some savage type. On atavism the Machine can have no mercy.

"There was a handle, and I did catch it. I hung tranced over the darkness and heard the hum of these workings as the last whisper in a dying dream. All the things I had cared about and all the people I had spoken to through tubes appeared infinitely little. Meanwhile the handle revolved. My weight had set something in motion and I span slowly, and then--

"I cannot describe it. I was lying with my face to the sunshine. Blood poured from my nose and ears and I heard a tremendous roaring. The stopper, with me clinging to it, had simply been blown out of the earth, and the air that we make down here was escaping through the vent into the air above. It burst up like a fountain. I crawled back to it—for the upper air hurts—and, as it were, I took great sips from the edge. My respirator had flown goodness knows here, my clothes were torn. I just lay with my lips close to the hole, and I sipped until the bleeding stopped. You can imagine nothing so curious. This hollow in the grass—I will speak of it in a minute,--the sun shining into it, not brilliantly but through marbled clouds,--the peace, the nonchalance, the sense of space, and, brushing my cheek, the roaring fountain of our artificial air! Soon I spied my respirator, bobbing up and down in the current high above my head, and higher still were many air-ships. But no one ever looks out of air-ships, and in any case they could not have picked me up. There I was, stranded. The sun shone a little way down the shaft, and revealed the topmost rung of the ladder, but it was hopeless trying to reach it. I should either have been tossed up again by the escape, or else have fallen in, and died. I could only lie on the grass, sipping and sipping, and from time to time glancing around me.

"I knew that I was in Wessex, for I had taken care to go to a lecture on the subject before starting. Wessex lies above the room in which we are talking now. It was once an important state. Its kings held all the southern coast form the Andredswald to Cornwall, while the Wansdyke protected them on the north, running over the high ground. The lecturer was only concerned with the rise of Wessex, so I do not know how long it remained an international power, nor would the knowledge have assisted me. To tell the truth I could do nothing but laugh, during this part. There was I, with a pneumatic stopper by my side and a respirator bobbing over my head, imprisoned, all three of us, in a grass-grown hollow that was edged with fern."

Then he grew grave again.

"Lucky for me that it was a hollow. For the air began to fall back into it and to fill it as water fills a bowl. I could crawl about. Presently I stood. I breathed a mixture, in which the air that hurts predominated whenever I tried to climb the sides. This was not so bad. I had not lost my tabloids and remained ridiculously cheerful, and as for the Machine, I forgot about it altogether. My one aim now was to get to the top, where the ferns were, and to view whatever objects lay beyond.

"I rushed the slope. The new air was still too bitter for me and I came rolling back, after a momentary vision of something grey. The sun grew very feeble, and I remembered that he was in Scorpio—I had been to a lecture on that too. If the sun is in Scorpio, and you are in Wessex, it means that you must be as quick as you can, or it will get too dark. (This is the first bit of useful information I have ever got from a lecture, and I expect it will be the last.) It made me try frantically to breathe the new air, and to advance as far as I dared out of my pond. The hollow filled so slowly. At times I thought that the fountain played with less vigour. My respirator seemed to dance nearer the earth; the roar was decreasing."

He broke off.

"I don't think this is interesting you. The rest will interest you even less. There are no ideas in it, and I wish that I had not troubled you to come. We are too different, mother."

She told him to continue.

"It was evening before I climbed the bank. The sun had very nearly slipped out of the sky by this time, and I could not get a good view. You, who have just crossed the Roof of the World, will not want to hear an account of the little hills that I saw—low colourless hills. But to me they were living and the turf that covered them was a skin, under which their muscles rippled, and I felt that those hills had called with incalculable force to men in the past, and that men had loved them. Now they sleep—perhaps for ever. They commune with humanity in dreams. Happy the man, happy the woman, who awakes the hills of Wessex. For though they sleep, they will never die."

His voice rose passionately.

"Cannot you see, cannot all you lecturers see, that it is we that are dying, and that down here the only thing that really lives in the Machine? We created the Machine, to do our will, but we cannot make it do our will now. It was robbed us of the sense of space and of the sense of touch, it has blurred every human relation and narrowed down love to a carnal act, it has paralyzed our bodies and our wills, and now it compels us to worship it. The Machine develops—but not on our lies. The Machine proceeds—but not to our goal. We only exist as the blood corpuscles that course through its arteries, and if it could work without us, it would let us die. Oh, I have no remedy—or, at least, only one—to tell men again and again that I have seen the hills of Wessex as Alfred saw them when he overthrew the Danes.

"So the sun set. I forgot to mention that a belt of mist lay between my hill and other hills, and that it was the colour of pearl."

He broke off for the second time.

"Go on," said his mother wearily.

He shook his head.

"Go on. Nothing that you say can distress me now. I am hardened."

"I had meant to tell you the rest, but I cannot; I know that I cannot; good-bye."

Vashti stood irresolute. All her nerves were tingling with his blasphemies. But she was also inquisitive.

"This is unfair," she complained. "You have called me across the world to hear your story, and hear it I will. Tell me—as briefly as possible, for this is a disastrous waste of time—tell me how you returned to civilization."

"Oh—that!" he said, starting. "You would like to hear about civilization. Certainly. Had I got to where my respirator fell down?"

"No—but I understand everything now. You put on your respirator, and managed to walk along the surface of the earth to a vomitory, and there your conduct was reported to the Central Committee."

"By no means."

He passed his hand over his forehead, as if dispelling some strong impression. Then, resuming his narrative, he warmed to it again.

"My respirator fell about sunset. I had mentioned that the fountain seemed feebler, had I not?" "Yes."

"About sunset, it let the respirator fall. As I said, I had entirely forgotten about the Machine, and I paid no great attention at the time, being occupied with other things. I had my pool of air, into which I could dip when the outer keenness became intolerable, and which would possibly remain for days, provided that no wind sprang up to disperse it. Not until it was too late did I realize what the stoppage of the escape implied. You see—the gap in the tunnel had been mended; the Mending Apparatus; the Mending Apparatus, was after me.

"One other warning I had, but I neglected it. The sky at night was clearer than it had been in the day, and the moon, which was about half the sky behind the sun, shone into the dell at moments quite brightly. I was in my usual place—on the boundary between the two atmospheres—when I thought I saw something dark move across the bottom of the dell, and vanish into the shaft. In my folly, I ran down. I bent over and listened, and I thought I heard a faint scraping noise in the depths.

"At this—but it was too late—I took alarm. I determined to put on my respirator and to walk right out of the dell. But my respirator had gone. I knew exactly where it had fallen—between the stopper and the aperture—and I could even feel the mark that it had made in the turf. It had gone, and I realized that something evil was at work, and I had better escape to the other air, and, if I must die, die running towards the cloud that had been the colour of a pearl. I never started.

146

Out of the shaft—it is too horrible. A worm, a long white worm, had crawled out of the shaft and gliding over the moonlit grass.

"I screamed. I did everything that I should not have done, I stamped upon the creature instead of flying from it, and it at once curled round the ankle. Then we fought. The worm let me run all over the dell, but edged up my leg as I ran. 'Help!' I cried. (That part is too awful. It belongs to the part that you will never know.) 'Help!' I cried. (Why cannot we suffer in silence?) 'Help!' I cried. When my feet were wound together, I fell, I was dragged away from the dear ferns and the living hills, and past the great metal stopper (I can tell you this part), and I thought it might save me again if I caught hold of the handle. It also was enwrapped, it also. Oh, the whole dell was full of the things. They were searching it in all directions, they were denuding it, and the white snouts of others peeped out of the hole, ready if needed. Everything that could be moved they brought—brushwood, bundles of fern, everything, and down we all went intertwined into hell. The last things that I saw, ere the stopper closed after us, were certain stars, and I felt that a man of my sort lived in the sky. For I did fight, I fought till the very end, and it was only my head hitting against the ladder that quieted me. I woke up in this room. The worms had vanished. I was surrounded by artificial air, artificial light, artificial peace, and my friends were calling to me down speaking-tubes to know whether I had come across any new ideas lately."

Here his story ended. Discussion of it was impossible, and Vashti turned to go. "It will end in Homelessness," she said quietly.

"I wish it would," retorted Kuno.

"The Machine has been most merciful."

"I prefer the mercy of God."

"By that superstitious phrase, do you mean that you could live in the outer air?"

"Yes."

"Have you ever seen, round the vomitories, the bones of those who were extruded after the Great Rebellion?"

"Yes."

"Have you ever seen, round the vomitories, the bones of those who were extruded after the Great Rebellion?"

"Yes."

"They were left where they perished for our edification. A few crawled away, but they perished, too—who can doubt it? And so with the Homeless of our own day. The surface of the earth supports life no longer."

"Indeed."

"Ferns and a little grass may survive, but all higher forms have perished. Has any air-ship detected them?" "No."

"Has any lecturer dealt with them?"

"No."

15

"Then why this obstinacy?"

"Because I have seen them," he exploded.

"Seen what?"

"Because I have seen her in the twilight—because she came to my help when I called—because she, too, was entangled by the worms, and, luckier than I, was killed by one of them piercing her throat."

He was mad. Vashti departed, nor, in the troubles that followed, did she ever see his face again.

III
THE HOMELESS

During the years that followed Kuno's escapade, two important developments took place in the Machine. On the surface they were revolutionary, but in either case men's minds had been prepared beforehand, and they did but express tendencies that were latent already.

The first of these was the abolition of respirator.

Advanced thinkers, like Vashti, had always held it foolish to visit the surface of the earth. Air-ships might be necessary, but what was the good of going out for mere curiosity and crawling along for a mile or two in a terrestrial motor? The habit was vulgar and perhaps faintly improper: it was unproductive of ideas, and had no connection with the habits that really mattered. So respirators were abolished, and with them, of course, the terrestrial motors, and except for a few lecturers, who complained that they were debarred access to their subject-matter, the development was accepted quietly. Those who still wanted to know what the earth was like had after all only to listen to some gramophone, or to look into some cinematophote. And even the lecturers acquiesced when they found that a lecture on the sea was none the less stimulating when compiled out of other lectures that had already been delivered on the same subject. "Beware of first-hand ideas!" exclaimed one of the most advanced of them. "First-hand ideas do not really exist. They are but the physical impressions produced by live and fear, and on this gross foundation who could erect a philosophy? Let your ideas be second-hand, and if possible tenth-hand, for then they will be far removed from that disturbing element--direct observation. Do not learn anything about this subject of mine—the French Revolution. Learn instead what I think that Enicharmon thought Urizen thought Gutch thought Ho-Yung thought Chi-Bo-Sing thought LafcadioHearn thought Carlyle thought Mirabeau said about the French Revolution. Through the medium of these ten great minds, the blood that was shed at Paris and the windows that were broken at Versailles will be clarified to an idea which you may employ most profitably in your daily lives. But be sure that the intermediates are many and varied, for in history one authority exists to counteract another. Urizen must counteract the skepticism of Ho-Yung and Enicharmon, I must myself counteract the impetuosity of Gutch. You who listen to me are in a better position to judge about the French Revolution than I am. Your descendants will be even in a better position than you, for they will learn what you think I think, and yet another intermediate will be added to the chain. And in time"--his voice rose--"there will come a generation that had got beyond facts, beyond impressions, a generation absolutely colourless, a generation seraphically free from taint of personality, which will see the French Revolution not as it happened, nor as they would like it to have happened, but as it would have happened, had it taken place in the days of the Machine."

Tremendous applause greeted this lecture, which did but voice a feeling already latent in the minds of men—a feeling that terrestrial facts must be ignored, and that the abolition of respirators was a positive gain. It was even suggested that air-ships should be abolished too. This was not done, because air-ships had somehow worked themselves into the Machine's system. But year by year they were used less, and mentioned less by thoughtful men.

The second great development was the re-establishment of religion.

This, too, had been voiced in the celebrated lecture. No one could mistake the reverent tone in which the peroration had concluded, and it awakened a responsive echo in the heart of each. Those who had long worshipped silently, now began to talk. They described the strange feeling of peace that came over them when they handled the Book of the Machine, the pleasure that it was to repeat certain numerals out of it, however little meaning those numerals conveyed to the outward ear, the ecstasy of touching a button, however unimportant, or of ringing an electric bell, however superfluously.

"The Machine," they exclaimed, "feeds us and clothes us and houses us; through it we speak to one another, through it we see one another, in it we have our being. The Machine is the friend of ideas and the enemy of superstition: the Machine is omnipotent, eternal; blessed is the Machine." And before long this allocution was printed on the first page of the Book, and in subsequent editions the ritual swelled into a complicated system of praise and prayer. The word "religion" was sedulously avoided, and in theory the Machine was still the creation and the implement of man, but in practice all, save a few retrogrades, worshipped it as divine. Nor was it worshipped in unity. One believer would be chiefly impressed by the blue optic plates, through which he saw other believers; another by the mending apparatus, which sinful Kuno had compared to worms; another by the lifts, another by the Book. And each would pray to this or to that, and ask it to intercede for him with the Machine as a whole. Persecution—that also was present. It did not break out, for reasons that will be set forward shortly. But it was latent, and all who did not accept the minimum known as "undenominational Mechanism" lived in danger of Homelessness, which means death, as we know.

To attribute these two great developments to the Central Committee, is to take a very narrow view of civilization. The Central Committee announced the developments, it is true, but they were no more the cause of them than were the kings of the imperialistic period the cause of war. Rather did they yield to some invincible pressure, which came no one knew whither, and which, when gratified, was succeeded by some new pressure equally invincible. To such a state of affairs it is convenient to give the name of progress. No one confessed the Machine was out of hand. Year by year it was served with increased efficiency and decreased intelligence. The better a man knew his own duties upon it, the less he understood the duties of his neighbour, and in all the world there was not one who understood the monster as a whole. Those master brains had perished. They had left full directions, it is true, and their successors had each of them mastered a portion of those directions. But Humanity, in its desire for comfort, had over-reached itself. It had exploited the riches of nature too far. Quietly and complacently, it was sinking into decadence, and progress had come to mean the progress of the Machine.

As for Vashti, her life went peacefully forward until the final disaster. She made her room dark and slept; she awoke and made the room light. She lectured and attended lectures. She exchanged ideas with her innumerable friends and believed she was growing more spiritual. At times a friend was granted Euthanasia, and left his or her room for the homelessness that is beyond all human conception. Vashti did not much mind. After an unsuccessful lecture, she would sometimes ask for Euthanasia herself. But the death-rate was not permitted to exceed the birth-rate, and the Machine had hitherto refused it to her.

The troubles began quietly, long before she was conscious of them.

One day she was astonished at receiving a message from her son. They never communicated, having nothing in common, and she had only heard indirectly that he was still alive, and had been transferred from the northern hemisphere, where he had behaved so mischievously, to the southern—indeed, to a room not far from her own.

"Does he want me to visit him?" she thought. "Never again, never. And I have not the time." No, it was madness of another kind.

He refused to visualize his face upon the blue plate, and speaking out of the darkness with solemnity said:

"The Machine stops."

"What do you say?"

"The Machine is stopping, I know it, I know the signs."

She burst into a peal of laughter. He heard her and was angry, and they spoke no more.

"Can you imagine anything more absurd?" she cried to a friend. "A man who was my son believes that the Machine is stopping. It would be impious if it was not mad."

"The Machine is stopping?" her friend replied. "What does that mean? The phrase conveys nothing to me." "Nor to me."

"He does not refer, I suppose, to the trouble there has been lately with the music?"

"Oh no, of course not. Let us talk about music."

"Have you complained to the authorities?"

"Yes, and they say it wants mending, and referred me to the Committee of the Mending Apparatus. I complained of those curious gasping sighs that disfigure the symphonies of the Brisbane school. They sound like some one in pain. The Committee of the Mending Apparatus say that it shall be remedied shortly."

Obscurely worried, she resumed her life. For one thing, the defect in the music irritated her. For another thing, she could not forget Kuno's speech. If he had known that the music was out of repair—he could not know it, for he detested music—if he had known that it was wrong, "the Machine stops" was exactly the venomous sort of remark he would have made. Of course he had made it at a venture, but the coincidence annoyed her, and she spoke with some petulance to the Committee of the Mending Apparatus.

They replied, as before, that the defect would be set right shortly.

"Shortly! At once!" she retorted. "Why should I be worried by imperfect music? Things are always put right at once. If you do not mend it at once, I shall complain to the Central Committee."

"No personal complaints are received by the Central Committee," the Committee of the Mending Apparatus replied.

"Through whom am I to make my complaint, then?" "Through us."

"I complain then."

"Your complaint shall be forwarded in its turn." "Have others complained?"

This question was unmechanical, and the Committee of the

Mending Apparatus refused to answer it.

"It is too bad!" she exclaimed to another of her friends.

"There never was such an unfortunate woman as myself. I can never be sure of my music now. It gets worse and worse each time I summon it."

"What is it?"

"I do not know whether it is inside my head, or inside the wall."

"Complain, in either case."

"I have complained, and my complaint will be forwarded in its turn to the Central Committee."

Time passed, and they resented the defects no longer. The defects had not been remedied, but the human tissues in that latter day had become so subservient, that they readily adapted themselves to every caprice of the Machine. The sigh at the crises of the Brisbane symphony no longer irritated Vashti; she accepted it as part of the melody. The jarring noise, whether in the head or in the wall, was no longer resented by her friend. And so with the mouldy artificial fruit, so with the bath water that began to stink, so with the defective rhymes that the poetry machine had taken to emit, all were bitterly complained of at first, and then acquiesced in and forgotten. Things went from bad to worse unchallenged.

It was otherwise with the failure of the sleeping apparatus. That was a more serious stoppage. There came a day when over the whole world—in Sumatra, in Wessex, in the innumerable cities of Courland and Brazil—the beds, when summoned by their tired owners, failed to appear. It may seem a ludicrous matter, but from it we may date the collapse of humanity. The Committee responsible for the failure was assailed by complainants, whom it referred, as usual, to the Committee of the Mending Apparatus, who in its turn assured them that their complaints would be forwarded to the Central Committee. But the discontent grew, for mankind was not yet sufficiently adaptable to do without sleeping.

"Some one of meddling with the Machine---" they began.

"Some one is trying to make himself king, to reintroduce the personal element."

"Punish that man with Homelessness."

CHRIS BIRD

"To the rescue! Avenge the Machine! Avenge the Machine!"

"War! Kill the man!"

But the Committee of the Mending Apparatus now came forward, and allayed the panic with well-chosen words. It confessed that the Mending Apparatus was itself in need of repair.

The effect of this frank confession was admirable.

"Of course," said a famous lecturer—he of the French Revolution, who gilded each new decay with splendour--"of course we shall not press our complaints now. The Mending Apparatus has treated us so well in the past that we all sympathize with it, and will wait patiently for its recovery. In its own good time it will resume its duties. Meanwhile let us do without our beds, our tabloids, our other little wants. Such, I feel sure, would be the wish of the Machine."

Thousands of miles away his audience applauded. The Machine still linked them. Under the seas, beneath the roots of the mountains, ran the wires through which they saw and heard, the enormous eyes and ears that were

their heritage, and the hum of many workings clothed their thoughts in one garment of subserviency. Only the old and the sick remained ungrateful, for it was rumoured that Euthanasia, too, was out of order, and that pain had reappeared among men.

It became difficult to read. A blight entered the atmosphere and dulled its luminosity. At times Vashti could scarcely see across her room. The air, too, was foul. Loud were the complaints, impotent the remedies, heroic the tone of the lecturer as he cried: "Courage! courage! What matter so long as the Machine goes on? To it the darkness and the light are one." And though things improved again after a time, the old brilliancy was never recaptured, and humanity never recovered from its entrance into twilight. There was a hysterical talk of "measures," of "provisional dictatorship," and the inhabitants of Sumatra were asked to familiarize themselves with the workings of the central power station, the said power station being situated in France. But for the most part panic reigned, and men spent their strength praying to their Books, tangible proofs of the Machine's omnipotence. There were gradations of terror—at times came rumours of hope—the Mending Apparatus was almost mended—the enemies of the Machine had been got under—new "nerve-centres" were evolving which would do the work even more magnificently than before. But there came a day when, without the slightest warning, without any previous hint of feebleness, the entire communication-system broke down, all over the world, and the world, as they understood it, ended.

Vashti was lecturing at the time and her earlier remarks had been punctuated with applause. As she proceeded the audience became silent, and at the conclusion there was no sound. Somewhat displeased, she called to a friend who was a specialist in sympathy. No sound: doubtless the friend was sleeping. And so with the next friend whom she tried to summon, and so with the next, until she remembered Kuno's cryptic remark, "The Machine stops".

The phrase still conveyed nothing. If Eternity was stopping it would of course be set going shortly.

For example, there was still a little light and air—the atmosphere had improved a few hours previously. There was still the Book, and while there was the Book there was security.

Then she broke down, for with the cessation of activity came an unexpected terror—silence.

She had never known silence, and the coming of it nearly killed her--- it did kill many thousands of people outright. Ever since her birth she had been surrounded by the steady hum. It was to the ear what artificial air was to the lungs, and agonizing pains shot across her head. And scarcely knowing what she did, she stumbled forward and pressed the unfamiliar button, the one that opened the door of her cell.

Now the door of the cell worked on a simple hinge of its own. It was not connected with the central power station, dying far away in France. It opened, rousing immoderate hopes in Vashti, for she thought that the Machine had been mended. It opened, and she saw the dim tunnel that curved far away towards freedom. One look, and then she shrank back. For the tunnel was full of people—she was almost the last in that city to have taken alarm.

People at any time repelled her, and these were nightmares from her worst dreams. People were crawling about, people were screaming, whimpering, gasping for breath, touching each other, vanishing in the dark, and ever and anon being pushed off the platform on to the live rail. Some were fighting round the electric bells, trying to summon trains which could not be summoned. Others were yelling for Euthanasia or for respirators, or blaspheming the Machine. Others stood at the doors of their cells fearing, like herself, either to stop in them or to leave them. And behind all the uproar was silence—the silence which is the voice of the earth and of the generations who have gone.

No—it was worse than solitude. She closed the door again and sat down to wait for the end. The disintegration went on, accompanied by horrible cracks and rumbling. The valves that restrained the Medical Apparatus

must have weakened, for it ruptured and hung hideously from the ceiling. The floor heaved and fell and flung her from the chair. A tube oozed towards her serpent fashion. And at last the final horror approached—light began to ebb, and she knew that civilization's long day was closing.

She whirled around, praying to be saved from this, at any rate, kissing the Book, pressing button after button. The uproar outside was increasing, and even penetrated the wall. Slowly the brilliancy of her cell was dimmed, the reflections faded from the metal switches. Now she could not see the reading-stand, now not the Book, though she held it in her hand. Light followed the flight of sound, air was following light, and the original void returned to the cavern from which it has so long been excluded. Vashti continued to whirl, like the devotees of an earlier religion, screaming, praying, striking at the buttons with bleeding hands.

It was thus that she opened her prison and escaped—escaped in the spirit: at least so it seems to me, ere my meditation closes. That she escapes in the body—I cannot perceive that. She struck, by chance, the switch that released the door, and the rush of foul air on her skin, the loud throbbing whispers in her ears, told her that she was facing the tunnel again, and that tremendous platform on which she had seen men fighting. They were not fighting now. Only the whispers remained, and the little whimpering groans. They were dying by hundreds out in the dark.

She burst into tears.

Tears answered her.

They wept for humanity, those two, not for themselves. They

could not bear that this should be the end. Ere silence was completed their hearts were opened, and they knew what had been important on the earth. Man, the flower of all flesh, the noblest of all creatures visible, man who had once made god in his image, and had mirrored his strength on the constellations, beautiful naked man was dying, strangled in the garments that he had woven. Century after century had he toiled, and here was his reward. Truly the garment had seemed heavenly at first, shot with colours of culture, sewn with the threads of self-denial. And heavenly it had been so long as man could shed it at will and live by the essence that is his soul, and the essence, equally divine, that is his body. The sin against the body— it was for that they wept in chief; the centuries of wrong against the muscles and the nerves, and those five portals by which we can alone apprehend—glozing it over with talk of evolution, until the body was white pap, the home of ideas as colourless, last sloshy stirrings of a spirit that had grasped the stars.

"Where are you?" she sobbed. His voice in the darkness said, "Here."

Is there any hope, Kuno?"

"None for us."

"Where are you?"

She crawled over the bodies of the dead. His blood spurted over her hands. "Quicker," he gasped, "I am dying—but we touch, we talk, not through the Machine." He kissed her.

"We have come back to our own. We die, but we have recaptured life, as it was in Wessex, when Alfred overthrew the Danes. We know what they know outside, they who dwelt in the cloud that is the colour of a pearl."

"But Kuno, is it true? Are there still men on the surface of the earth? Is this--- tunnel, this poisoned darkness--- really not the end?"

He replied:

"I have seen them, spoken to them, loved them. They are hiding in the midst and the ferns until our civilization stops. Today they are the Homeless--- tomorrow ---"

"Oh, tomorrow--- some fool will start the Machine again, tomorrow." "Never," said Kuno, "never. Humanity has learnt its lesson."

As he spoke, the whole city was broken like a honeycomb. An air-ship had sailed in through the vomitory into a ruined wharf. It crashed downwards, exploding as it went, rending gallery after gallery with its wings of steel. For a moment they saw the nations of the dead, and, before they joined them, scraps of the untainted sky.

TOBEY A. ANDERSON

160

Made in the USA
San Bernardino, CA
23 March 2015